**Praise for the Novels and Stories of
Tod Goldberg
Finalist for the *Los Angeles Times* Book Prize**

"A keen voice, profound insight . . . devilishly entertaining." —*Los Angeles Times*

"Goldberg's prose is deceptively smooth, like a vanilla milk shake spiked with grain alcohol."
—*Chicago Tribune*

"[A] creepy, strangely sardonic, definitely disturbing version of Middle America . . . and that, of course, is where the fun begins." —*LA Weekly*

"Perfect . . . with all the sleaze and glamour of the old paperbacks of fifty years ago."—*Kirkus Reviews*

"Striking and affecting . . . Goldberg is a gifted writer, poetic and rigorous . . . a fiction tour de force . . . a haunting book." —January Magazine

Praise for the Series

"Likably lighthearted and cool as a smart-mouthed loner . . . cheerfully insouciant."
—*The New York Times*

continued . . .

burn notice
The End Game

TOD GOLDBERG

Based on the USA Network Television Series

Created by Matt Nix

AN OBSIDIAN MYSTERY

OBSIDIAN
Published by New American Library, a division of
Penguin Group (USA) Inc., 375 Hudson Street,
New York, New York 10014, USA
Penguin Group (Canada), 90 Eglinton Avenue East, Suite 700, Toronto,
Ontario M4P 2Y3, Canada (a division of Pearson Penguin Canada Inc.)
Penguin Books Ltd., 80 Strand, London WC2R 0RL, England
Penguin Ireland, 25 St. Stephen's Green, Dublin 2,
Ireland (a division of Penguin Books Ltd.)
Penguin Group (Australia), 250 Camberwell Road,
Camberwell, Victoria 3124,
Australia (a division of Pearson Australia Group Pty. Ltd.)
Penguin Books India Pvt. Ltd., 11 Community Centre, Panchsheel Park,
New Delhi - 110 017, India
Penguin Group (NZ), 67 Apollo Drive, Rosedale, North Shore 0632,
New Zealand (a division of Pearson New Zealand Ltd.)
Penguin Books (South Africa) (Pty.) Ltd., 24 Sturdee Avenue,
Rosebank, Johannesburg 2196, South Africa

Penguin Books Ltd., Registered Offices:
80 Strand, London WC2R 0RL, England

First published by Obsidian, an imprint of New American Library,
a division of Penguin Group (USA) Inc.

First Printing, May 2009
10 9 8 7 6 5 4 3

For Wendy, who always inspires me to be better.

ACKNOWLEDGMENTS

As ever, I am grateful to Matt Nix for letting me play with his toys. Extra-special thanks to Rashad Raisani for listening to my story and telling me a better one. Thanks also to: my brother, Lee Goldberg, for midnight support and wise counsel; my agent, Jennie Dunham, for her constant faith; my ever-patient editor, Kristen Weber, for being ever-patient; and my wife, Wendy, without whom these pages would be blank.

Much thanks for helpful research hints: Walt Stone, Dan Jimenez, Timothy Schmand and Ryan Johnson. Since I am not a spy, I'd encourage all of you to avoid doing anything in this book that might cause you to blow up—besides, I make a lot of stuff up. However, if you want to read about the real folks, I found the following books very enlightening from a research standpoint: *Marine Force Recon* by Fred J. Pushies, *Why Spy: Espionage in an Age of Uncertainty* and *The Great Game: Myths and Reality of Espionage*, both by Frederick Hitz.

I

When you're a spy, the word *belated* gets eradicated from your vocabulary. You don't send belated birthday cards. You don't send belated Christmas cards. You don't send belated wedding, anniversary, graduation or congratulations cards. You don't even bother to send belated wishes via e-mail. You tend to miss physical events like birthdays and baptisms and Bar Mitzvahs, because it's nearly impossible to tell a Taliban assassin you'll have to halt his inquisition until Monday so you can make it to T.G.I. Friday's for your buddy's fortieth.

If birthdays, weddings and holidays meant a lot to you, you wouldn't be traveling the world under diplomatic cloak; you'd be sitting in a cubicle, rigging the Secret Santa lottery, drafting memos about the need for casual Fridays, and fantasizing about the person who services the photocopier. Being a spy means never being forced to eat potato skins in a T.G.I. Friday's surrounded by men in Dockers or expressing your emotions through the mystery of Hallmark.

When you're no longer a spy, however, you learn pretty quickly that there's no card that says, *Sorry I missed the last dozen Mother's Days. I was busy doing black ops.* And yet there I was, in the middle of Target in midtown Miami, staring at row after row of greeting cards, trying to find one that might justifiably say that very thing.

My ex-girlfriend/former IRA operative/current business associate/confusing-person-of-romantic-interest Fiona Glenanne handed me a card. "This one is cute," she said.

The cover read: *I'm Sorry* . . . The inside said: . . . *For being a terrible son. Happy Mother's Day!*

"Subtle," I said.

"I think it would speak to your mother." She handed me another card. This one had a photo of a line of identical puppies trailing behind their mother. On the inside it said: *It could have been worse. There could have been ten just like me. Happy Mother's Day!*

"A lovely sentiment," I said. "But no."

"Have you thought about composing your own card?"

"Fi," I said, "I don't even want to *buy* a card. Why would I want to *make* one?"

"I don't know, Michael," Fiona said. "Maybe to show your mother you appreciate her carrying your vile existence for nine months."

She had a point. The problem was that if I started making my mother handmade Mother's Day cards now, next year at this time expectations would be astronomical, and next year I planned on being out of Miami permanently. It may be a big city, but when you're essentially trapped in the city limits by your own government, every day it seems to shrink by an inch.

One moment, I was a covert operative in fine standing, negotiating a wire transfer with a Russian gangster over a Nigerian oil refinery. The next moment, I was an ex–covert operative in exceptionally poor status, running for my life. Subsequently, I've been ensnared here, in Miami, trying to figure out the truth behind who issued my burn notice, thus placing me on a blacklist the world over, my movements alternately watched by the FBI and ignored by the FBI. As long as I don't leave the surrounding area, I won't heat up. So for the last year, I've been forced to take jobs helping people while I try to gather evidence on the people who turned my dossier into a bible of lies, learning along the way that I've been moved like a pawn and how difficult it is to find the king.

That's the easy part compared to navigating my mother Madeline's emotional ballistics. I've spent nearly forty years on this planet, have dodged bullets and missiles, have killed men, have blown up buildings, have found myself disavowed by my own government. . . . And I would do all of those things again, twice even, if it meant I wouldn't need to find an appropriate Mother's Day card.

"Why don't I just take her out to dinner?" I said.

"You should *make* her dinner," Fi said, and handed me another card. "This one is nice."

On the front was a huge mushroom cloud erupting over a '50s-era tract home. I didn't bother to open it up. "This isn't, technically, helping," I said.

"Suit yourself," she said. "I'm going to the garden section. See if they might have anything I can later use to incinerate your loft when you invariably disappoint me again."

"That sounds like a great plan," I said.

I watched Fiona walk away. Both men and women followed her as she passed. She paused for a moment in front of a display of scented candles, let her fingers idle on one, leaned forward to smell it, like she was putting on a little show, letting people know she was in the building, in case anyone hadn't noticed her yet.

A Cuban kid wearing a wife beater and with a barbed-wire tattoo that climbed up the middle of his throat stopped behind her and ogled her ass. He didn't realize it, but depending upon Fiona's mood, he was potentially about five seconds away from losing a vital organ.

Fi must have been in a good mood, since when she turned around and saw the kid she just smiled and whisked away.

She had that *thing*. There wasn't anything physically imposing about her—she was small, really, barely over 5'3", maybe weighed a hundred pounds with a gun strapped to her ankle—but she walked like a panther, carried herself with a confidence that said she could sleep with you or kill you and it really made no difference to her which outcome won. In a different world, I suppose it would be a lot easier to just be with Fiona, but there's nothing easy about being in a relationship with someone recognized as an international criminal, particularly when you're a spy. Or used to be a spy. My own identity crises probably didn't help the situation.

I spent the next ten minutes thumbing through cards. None of them appealed to me. I kept looking for one that said something along the lines of *I love you, despite it all*, but Hallmark didn't seem to have that one available this season.

Things were getting dire. I called my younger brother, Nate, to see what he was planning on doing. He answered on the fifteenth ring.

"Bro, if someone doesn't answer after five rings, that means they aren't home," Nate said. He sounded like he'd been sleeping. For days.

"What are you getting Ma for Mother's Day?" I said.

"You don't say hello?"

"I thought you weren't home," I said. "I was leaving a message."

"What time is it?"

"Eleven thirty."

"Crap," he said. "I'm late."

"Where do you ever have to be?"

"I've got appointments," he said. "People depend on me."

Nate has never had a real job. Doesn't have a real job. Will never have a real job. He periodically drives a limo, which isn't a real job. Driving all day and getting nowhere does not qualify as actual work. Even a hamster would agree. I suspect one day the IRS will want to have a long, involved chat with him.

"You driving to jai alai or the track?"

"If you must know, jai alai," Nate said. "And then I have a few drops at Indian casinos."

"You running people or bets?"

"I have a vested interest in the success of the sport and in the gambling industry as a way of helping the Native Americans."

"It's Mother's Day, Nate," I said.

"When has that ever mattered to you?"

"I'm just saying," I said. "Listen. I'm going blind staring at cards. Tell me what you got Ma and I'll let you go."

"The same thing I get her every year."

Dealing with Nate is often a delicate exercise. He doesn't react well to authority. He also doesn't think of me as authority, which compounds things. "Right," I said. I picked up another card. This one featured a picture of a morbidly obese woman in a bikini. The inside said: *I might be responsible for your stretch marks, but at least you're not this fat. Happy Mother's Day!* "When did greeting cards get so mean?"

"Where are you?" Nate said.

"Target."

"Aren't you all domesticated now?"

"I even eat with silverware. You were about to tell me what you got Ma."

"If you had a yard, you could get one of those blow-up pools. Get Sam to play lifeguard to the neighborhood kids. He was a SEAL, right?"

Nate was talking about Sam Axe, my de facto watchdog and partner, who was indeed a SEAL, but was now essentially Jimmy Buffett with a license to kill.

"Not likely. Listen. I need you to focus. What did you get Ma?"

"Maybe Fiona could take up baking," Nate said.

"Are you done yet?"

"Oh, I could go all day."

"Just tell me what I need to know and I'll let you back to your life of leisure and won't even tell Fi about that baking remark. Save us all a lot of problems."

Nate said, "You're the spy. Figure it out." And then he hung up. I called him back, but after twenty rings I figured he'd made his point.

A woman wearing an outfit made entirely of

pink and green terry cloth pulled her cart up beside me and started leafing through the cards. She was about my mother's age, maybe a few years older, and she smelled vaguely of cigarettes and a floral perfume that immediately made my head hurt.

When you're in a hot zone and aren't sure of local custom, it's wise to capture and interrogate someone who will give you the information you need to survive. Better to deal with certainty than to be the victim of assumed intel.

"Pardon me," I said, and when the woman turned to regard me, I smiled at her with all the gusto I could manage. "What's your name, ma'am?"

"Evelyn."

"Evelyn, if you were my mother, what would you want for Mother's Day?"

Evelyn pondered my question for a moment and then brightened up. "A Crock-Pot."

"Really?"

"Absolutely. Or a toaster oven. Cost of gas these days, a toaster oven makes a lot of sense."

"What about in terms of cards?"

"Something with Snoopy. I've always liked Snoopy." She scanned the racks and then handed me a card with Snoopy grasping his chest with glee, little red hearts bursting all around him. On the inside it said, simply, *Happy Mother's Day*.

"Would I need to add anything to this? Some kind of salutation?"

Again Evelyn pondered silently before answering. "Well," she said, "you don't seem like someone who really knows how to express emotions very well. So I'd say no."

That sounded reasonable. "Good. Good. Great, actually. *Great*. You are correct. Snoopy card and a toaster oven. Precisely." And here I pointed. I'm not sure why, but it made me feel less like an emotionless cyborg that even a woman caped in terry cloth could see through.

"Is this some kind of contest?" Evelyn said. "Have I won something?"

"Yes," I said. "Yes. Absolutely." I took Evelyn's hand and shook it vigorously. "You have indeed. Target thanks you for your support. Everything in the store is twenty percent off. Enjoy. Happy Mother's Day."

After the woman skittered off to shop to her heart's content, the entire world 20 percent brighter and filled with more possibility, I finally located the appliance aisle about a city block away and grabbed a silver toaster oven and a matching silver Crock-Pot, figuring, What the hell? Might as well come big.

It was still odd for me to be walking through a place like Target without feeling like there was an actual target on my back. You spend the majority of your life in foreign countries, taking care of other people's problems, you tend to feel a tad claustrophobic in an enormous box with only one marked exit, never mind that seeing so many people wearing red uniforms made me think I was being tracked by the Coldstream Guards.

You either decompress quickly or you become a cautionary tale. I've known guys who, the moment they were decommissioned, began to think every letter was a letter bomb, every white powder was anthrax, every woman who showed even the slightest bit of interest in them was out to cut their throat for something they did when Germany still had a wall dividing it. Those guys got departure interviews, retirement packages and health benefits and still couldn't stop feeling it.

I got a burn notice, a one-way ticket to Miami and an open invitation across the world for people to come looking for me. One way or another, you either adapt or you died, literally, metaphorically, whatever.

This is why I should have immediately recognized David Harris, a kid I went to high school with, when he entered the small cooking appliance aisle.

I was busy pondering the existence of egg cookers in this world when I saw him. The exit behind me was blocked by a woman pushing a baby stroller. She and the baby stopped in front of a display of blenders and both seemed equally transfixed on the wonder of it all. Had I immediately recognized David, I could have knocked down the metal shelves on either side of me like dominoes and then sprinted over them and out of the store. I could have conceivably fired a couple shots into the air-conditioning unit humming above my head, which would cause a huge fireball to erupt in the interstate of ducts crisscrossing the store, and everyone would be so confused they'd have no idea who they thought they might have recognized from third-period science. I could have grabbed a can of PAM, lit a match and created a blowtorch.

But none of that happened.

"Mike? Mike Westen? *Westy*? Is that you?"

I looked at the man in front of me and tried to place him. He had a receding hairline that he tried to hide by keeping it cut close to his scalp, but he also had one of those Bimini islands in the middle of his head that made him look indecisive.

There is bald and there is not bald.

No in-between.

He hadn't figured that out yet.

He wore jeans and a Polo shirt, the real kind with the guy on the horse and everything, and a Rolex diving watch, though I had real doubts he'd ever been deeper than his backyard Jacuzzi. I noticed a bulge around his midsection that was hidden slightly by how high he wore his pants, but not by much. All of which gave me the sense that we didn't storm a weapons warehouse together in the Sunni Triangle.

"Nope," I said. "Wrong guy." I tried to push on

past him, but he'd angled his cart in such a way that I'd have to actually split the atom to get around him. It was a consideration.

"Do you remember me, Mike?" he asked. "David? Davey Harris? AYSO? Civics with Mr. Dunaway? Ringing any bells?"

Crap.

I'd made it a point to avoid running into anyone I might have grown up with, which is difficult when your hometown is a tourist mecca, never mind probably a decent place to spend your adult life provided you aren't a former spy on the run. Which I guess is probably a fairly small sample.

"I've got a slight case of tinnitus," I said, "bells are just outside my range."

He leaned over and slapped me on the back with a bit more enthusiasm than I was comfortable with. "Man, you still got it," he said. "I heard you were back in town but didn't believe it. I think the last time I saw you was the day before graduation. Remember? We got that party ball and sat on the fifty-yard line? I think it was you, me, Gordon, Zander, Coop, DeWitt and, I think, Roberts—who I just found on Facebook. You on Facebook, Mike?"

"No."

"Man, it's like a digital class reunion. You should get on there. Man. So good to see you." He reached over and pinched my stomach. "All trim and cut up, and here I am with this gut—real turn of the screw, eh, Westy? Not like the old days."

If he touched me once more, I was going to break his wrist. "Who told you I was in town?"

"Oh, my mom ran into your mom at Publix a couple months ago. Told her you were a spy or something crazy."

"Unbelievable," I said, because it truly was unbelievable. International crime syndicates would pay hard cash to get a bead on my movements, and all they needed to do was corner Ma at Publix. Maybe they'd been shopping at the Winn-Dixie and because of that had missed their opportunity completely.

"Yeah, well, parents, right?"

"Right."

An uncomfortable silence descended on Davey. As far as I was concerned, we'd covered all of the essentials of polite conversation and could therefore back away without residual injury, but I could tell that Davey was hoping for me to say something so he could start talking about himself, which would then lead to him giving me a business card and then maybe an offer to talk about my retirement portfolio, because guys like Davey Harris always knew something about retirement portfolios. The only thing I wanted to know was how a guy could go through life calling himself Davey.

The larger issue was that I could see Fiona walking up behind Davey, which meant that I was about thirty seconds from being in a situation beyond my control.

"What *do* you do these days, Westy?"

If he called me Westy again, there was going to be a problem.

"Kill people for the government," I said.

"Can you imagine? Be like James Bond, back when he was cool? I just got the whole Connery DVD set a couple weeks ago. My opinion? Lazenby could have been the best Bond."

"Look, David," I began, but Davey cut me off with a dismissive wave, which made me think breaking his wrist would be a favor to a lot of people.

"Davey. Everyone calls me Davey still."

"Right. *David*. No offense? But I don't remember you. I don't remember Gordon or Coop or DeWitt or any of the other guys you mentioned. I trust we went to school together, I really do, but I'm drawing a real blank here."

"We went to school together for *twelve years*, Mike. How can you not remember me?"

I could've told him the truth. I could've said that I'd probably replaced him in my mind with weapons training manuals for every gun produced foreign and domestically for the last twenty years. I could've told him that I needed the brain space occupied by all the memories of him and Coop for the schematics concerning how one best uses duct tape as a weapon. Or I could have told him that I'd forgotten him because I'd spent the last two decades trying to forget all I could about this place.

But then Fiona walked up and solved all of my problems.

"He's had a traumatic brain injury," she said. She swept around Davey, grazed him with her hip, which actually got him to move his cart a couple inches, something I'd been completely unable to manage, and then stood next to me. "He probably hasn't even mentioned me, has he?"

"No," Davey said, "he hasn't. A brain injury, Westy?"

"Traumatic brain injury," I said.

"Your mom didn't mention that. Man. That's awful."

"Yeah," I said.

"I'm sorry," Fiona said, "but I need to get . . . Westy . . . home before his medication wears off."

"Are you his nurse?"

This would be one of those days that would take me years to live down.

"Of a sort, I guess you could say," Fiona said, and then she shook Davey's hand in a very businesslike manner. "A pleasure to meet an old friend of . . . Westy's. But we must get going so . . . Westy . . . can have his fun time taking apart kitchen appliances before his darkness takes over, as I'm sure you know."

Davey had no idea what Fiona was saying, but by the end of the day, I suspected that anyone I went to high school with would have a fairly strong mental picture of me.

"Let me give you my card," Davey said to Fiona, his voice just above a whisper, as if I couldn't still hear him, as if he wasn't standing directly in front of me, "in case he ever needs any help planning for his future. Does he have any kind of retirement set up?"

2

You have two choices when facing a hostile interrogation: Tell the truth or tell a lie. The problem here is that if you're being interrogated by hostile forces, the end result is that you're likely going to be killed regardless. So in the event that you find yourself on the pointed end of a knife, or looking down the barrel of a gun, or are simply sitting in a bathtub filled with water while one guy wearing a mask holds a video camera and another a plugged-in hair dryer, each awaiting your confession, well, you give whatever answer you think will buy you a few more minutes to formulate an escape plan.

"So, you didn't have any friends, Michael?" Fiona asked.

"Not that I choose to recall," I said. We were in the Charger but not moving, traffic in midtown Miami having come to a complete stop. Now would be a good time to have an extraction team.

"Who did you eat lunch with?"

"I didn't," I said.

"You didn't eat, or you didn't eat with people?"

"I mostly did sit-ups."

"And who do you blame for this, your mother or your father?"

"Combination of both," I said. "What's with all this traffic?"

"After school, you didn't play with anyone?"

"No, I didn't play with anyone. I built a lot of things. Small explosives. My own BBs. That sort of thing."

"And where was Nate?"

"Causing problems somewhere," I said. I turned on the radio and searched for a station with a traffic report, but all I found were stations playing hip-hop and Gloria Estefan. Doesn't matter what station you listen to in Miami; they all play Gloria Estefan.

"Was I your first kiss, Michael?"

"Fi," I said.

"It occurs to me that Sam is the only friend of yours I've ever met," Fiona said.

"You met Larry," I said.

"Who wasn't really your friend," she said.

"He was for a while," I said.

"He was an assassin," she said.

"Well, before that, he had good points."

"Being an efficient killer doesn't count." I gave Fi a look. "Normally, anyway."

"You met Ricky," I said. "My friend Andre's kid brother."

"That's right. And where is Andre now?"

"Doing twenty-five," I said. "And now you have Davey. The five of you should go out and swap stories about me. Let me know what you find out."

We were on our way to South Beach to meet my mother—Fiona kindly phoned her from Target and told her we'd decided gifts just wouldn't do, and that I'd like to buy her dinner, as well—but the 195, the causeway we'd need to get on to get across the water, was frozen in front of us, too.

I made a left turn off Miami Avenue and wound around Roberto Clemente Park. Used to be this part of town was all working-class Puerto Rican families, but now it was this weird mix of big-box stores, high-rise condos, art galleries, coffeehouses, dollar stores, empty warehouses, boarded-up houses, chain-link fences, jungle gyms on broken pavement, cops parked window to window under trees and teenage gangsters trying to look hard, but mostly looking like they were bothered by the humidity and just wanted to be inside. I doubted any of them knew who Roberto Clemente was.

"You take me to the nicest places, Michael," Fiona said. The pleasant thing about being with Fiona is that you drive through a bad neighborhood with her and she doesn't lock the doors and scream for you to find the closest Quiznos. She just takes it all in. Cereal-box gangsters and graffiti scare her about as much as a guppy scares a shark.

She was looking out the window and smiling at the corner boys, periodically waving at them as we passed.

"You want to know what I did when I was a kid?" I said. "I came down here and stole cars. Half of them were already stolen or had fake plates as it was. Sometimes, Nate and I would steal a car here, drive it to the Pork 'n' Beans Projects, steal another car there, drive it back over here and then catch the bus back home before my dad even knew we were gone."

"And that was fun?"

"That was the best time," I said. "Better than being home, Fiona. Better than being home."

We wound back through 34th Street, picked up the 195 and circled back to the MacArthur Causeway, which was a longer trip, but I didn't mind too terribly much. I'd already seen my mother five times that week—once to unclog her sink, which it turns out was backed up with a compound of cigarette ash and animal fat, which had turned into a marcite-like substance in her disposal; once to take her to see her podiatrist in order to get her troublesome ingrown toenail cut out; once to assure her that her neighbors were not using their DirecTV unit to bug her conversations; once to show her how to operate her DVD player and once to dissuade her from making me go to family therapy with her again.

It was her new thing. She wanted us to get

closer to each other, to get past my anger at her having been married to my father, of her letting him treat us like leaves, something to be raked up and burnt, and to, as the last article she clipped from Oprah's magazine said, "mend our broken home."

Twenty years of psychological training in warfare and battle. Armed conflicts in half the world. Set up shadow governments in countries that don't even exist anymore. No one told me I'd still be responsible for repairing my past, too.

From the MacArthur Causeway I could see what was causing all the backup on the parallel causeway—a yacht the size of Bali had crashed into a piling beneath the Venetian Causeway, which runs between the MacArthur and the Tuttle. There wasn't any real damage to the causeway, as it looked to be a glancing blow, but the yacht seemed wedged into place. The water was filled with other boats, mostly other ostentatious yachts, as well as a series of rescue ships and Port Authority boats making their way towards the accident.

"What's with the luxury fleet?" I said. The bay was frequently filled with gorgeous boats and dinghies alike, but there was something clearly different on this day. Yachts like you only see on the coast of Italy and in rap videos were thick on the water, some so close to each other it was hard to distinguish where one began and the other ended.

"There's a race this week," Fi said. "One of those playboys-with-toys events."

"Why do you know that?"

"A business contact is coming into town for it," she said. "Do you have any pressing needs for weapons-grade plutonium?"

"No."

"Shame."

"Who do you know who is handling plutonium?" I said.

"Just an old playboy."

"Anyone I know?"

Fi tried to hide her smile, but I caught a glimpse of it. I am not a jealous person. I'm not. Normally. At all. In the least.

"He's very complex," she said. "Your complete opposite." It occurred to me that Fiona was probably making up this entire scenario as she went along. "Whereas you're cagey and apt to disappoint," she continued, "he is perfectly acute to everyone's feelings."

"Which is why he's trying to move weapons-grade plutonium."

"Everyone has bills, Michael."

Just as I was about to respond that it might be wise for Fiona to keep herself a safe distance from anyone handling plutonium, lest they be inexperienced with it and find themselves in a situation where they might accidentally kill everyone in a ten-mile radius, or at the very least give them all inoperable cancer, I was distracted by the explosion of the crashed yacht. One moment it was a ship; the next it was a thousand flaming splinters raining into Biscayne Bay and back onto the causeway. Within moments, the palm trees and slash pines that dot the causeway just east of the accident site burst into flames, paradise burning in mere seconds, the sky filling with ugly black smoke.

Most people live their entire lives without witnessing an explosion firsthand. That's because things rarely explode.

Things catch on fire.

Things burn down.

Things occasionally crash into other things and then ignite, but then stop burning after a short period of time.

In order for something to explode, two things generally need to be in place: a trigger and a person who wants to blow something up. Other than small children, you'd be surprised by how few people on this planet have a real desire to create widespread criminal destruction.

If you want to kill someone and get away with it, blowing up their yacht isn't the best way. If a boat is going to explode on its own, there will be evidence—leaking gas line, compromised fuses, a faulty battery. Any of these things could cause a boat to explode, provided there was a perfect and rare confluence of events. The key is that the explosion would come from the bottom up, where the gas, battery and fuses are kept.

Not, as even we could see paused on the causeway, from the flying bridge, unless the people driving the yacht kept high-powered accelerants there or were taking on mortar fire. None of which seemed the likely occurrence, even from our distant vantage point.

It wasn't my problem. And to some degree, that felt good.

Nevertheless, cars all around us came to a halt and passengers started hopping out to look at the wreckage, which is always a bad idea, but since everyone is now a "citizen journalist" they were willing to risk their lives to shoot shaky videos and wobbly photos from their cell phones. Fi and I just kept moving. Besides, we'd both seen worse. And neither of us wanted our picture taken.

"You know how your friend was making it into Miami?" I asked.

"Boat," Fi said.

"Big boat or small boat?"

"Big."

I nodded. "He already in town?"

"I hope so," she said.

"If there was weapons-grade plutonium in *that*," I said and pointed out the window, though we couldn't see the fire anymore, the MacArthur having turned south briefly, though smoke had filled the sky and sirens could be heard from all directions, "we'd already be dead. And that causeway would probably be gone, too."

"Your point?"

"No point," I said. "Just making a statement. Playboys don't know much about explosives, that's all."

"That seem peculiar to you?" Fiona said. "That boat exploding like that, all that smoke, fire, destruction?"

"The fact that it clearly was a bomb of some kind?"

"Yes, that," she said.

"Fi," I said, "it's Mother's Day. I can only be possessed by one disaster at a time."

"I'm not possessed by it," Fi said, "just noting that if, at some later point, you'd like to do something like that as you go about walking the earth helping the unfortunate, that it can be done with a lot less damage and does make for an impressive display of might. Just something to keep in your little head."

We drove on, but Fi's point was well made, even if I didn't listen. The other aspect of an explosion like that was if it turned out to be something truly awful or notable, eventually someone of importance would notice that Fi and I were in the vicinity, might even have access to a security photo of my car driving on the opposite causeway at the precise time of the explosion, since even if the public wasn't aware, subsequent to 9/11, most significant bridges and causeways now had surveillance cameras trained on each passing car and, invariably, I'd need to make an accounting or have it used against me.

The nice thing about being paranoid? It gets you to cover your ass when you might normally let it hang out in the open. Even though Sam was no longer regularly informing on me to the FBI, it was important to keep him abreast of potential issues that might arise in the event that I'm at some point implicated, along with Fi, in blowing up a million-dollar yacht.

So, after we hit Miami Beach, and after I called my mom to let her know we were running a little late because something had just blown up in Biscayne Bay, I dialed Sam. "Just if you're curious," I said when he answered, "that didn't have anything to do with me."

"What didn't?" he said.

I could hear talking in the background and dishes being gathered up. The clink of glasses. Silverware. I looked at my watch. It was about twelve thirty, which meant Sam had been at the Café Carlito for about two hours and five to seven beers. I doubted he was watching the news.

"Some yacht just went kaboom in the bay," I said.

"Funny thing," he said. "I just met with someone about a yacht."

"I know where you can get one cheap," I said. "Might need some work."

"A guy with a job," Sam said. "Needs some discreet help. I told him I knew just the person."

"How discreet is it if you tell everyone who asks?" This caused Sam to pause and think. While Sam has had to act as the eyes and ears on me for the government, it's more passive than aggressive. In fact, it's almost completely passive now. We have an agreement that he'll give the least he can and I won't imperil him more than I have to. It works about fifty percent of the time, and that's largely his fifty percent. "Fi and I are having lunch with my mother. Where are you going to be in an hour?"

"Training for a ten K," Sam said.

"So the Carlito?" I said.

"Unless they run out of limes," he said.

"Got it," I said.

"And you said a yacht blew up?"

"A big one."

"You see any Italians in expensive suits running from the scene?"

"I didn't see the scene," I said. "It was on the water."

"Well, good. What about in sweat suits?"

"Sam," I said, "have you agreed to help some mobbed-up pigeon?"

"No, no," he said.

"You're just keeping an eye out for Italians in expensive suits and track wear these days?"

"Give your mom my best," he said. "She and Virgil having a special day, too?"

Virgil was an old friend of Sam's who, inexplicably, took a shine to my mother after we twice helped him with special problems, once involving vicious drug dealers and once . . . well, involving another group of vicious drug dealers. Subsequently, he and my mother have had a thing. Not a thing like what Fiona and I have. Nor a thing I really want to consider, ever, or even a thing like my mother and father had, but a *thing* no less. You never want to think of your parents having a romantic life. It's the sort of thought process that makes therapy appointments even more uncomfortable.

It was also an excellent way of changing the subject. You deal with people with psy-ops training, you have to figure they'll occasionally put their training to use.

"Not that I'm aware of."

"Ah, Mikey, it's good for both of them. Just like that song said. Two less lonely people in the world," Sam said.

"I'm afraid I don't know that song."

"Little before your time. We tortured Noriega with it. Now it sort of runs in a loop in my head. Anyway, I think it's sweet. Have a laugh, Mikey—it's a funny situation."

"This is me laughing," I said, and hung up. We were driving down 5th Street and Fi told me to take a right on Collins, and then a brief left on 3rd Street, and then had me stop in front of a big red-striped edifice that made me wonder if my thoughts were somehow getting uploaded to a master computer that was transmitting directly to Fi and my mother.

"T.G.I. Friday's?" I said. "You told my mother to meet us at T.G.I. Friday's?"

"Your mother loves it," she said, "and they actually serve protein-based foods, so it will be a nice shock to your system."

As we walked into the restaurant, I tried to remember how we used to spend Mother's Day, back when Dad was still alive and Nate and I were still just kids, not whatever we are now. I had a vague memory of a trip north to Weeki Wachee Springs to see the mermaid show, another memory of Ma throwing a plate of frozen meat at Dad after he forgot to get her anything, another of us asking when kid's day was and her telling us that every day was kid's day, except that I don't precisely recall ever having a day that felt all that celebratory for being the kind of kid I was.

Ma sat at a table with a huge vase of flowers in the middle of it. She looked positively beatific in her glow. I couldn't remember the last time I saw her like that. When she saw us, she jumped up from the table and threw her arms around me.

"Oh, Michael," she said, "you shouldn't have."

"It was nothing," I said. I had no idea what she was talking about.

"It was just so unexpected," she said. She was still holding on to me as I tried to get to a seat at the table, so I sort of had to drag her a bit. "So thoughtful! How did you remember my favorite flowers?"

I looked down at the vase. It overflowed with pink lilies, a burst of yellow sunflowers and a sprinkling of light blue irises. "I don't know," I said, but then I saw the card affixed to the vase. It said, HAPPY MOTHER'S DAY, LOVE, MICHAEL & NATE.

"Oh, it's perfect," she said. "Such a surprise. I had to bring it from home so Fiona could see it. Isn't it lovely, Fiona? Isn't it a wonderful surprise? I didn't think he'd remember now that he's home."

"It sure is," Fi said.

When you're not a spy anymore, it's important to sometimes expect the best of people, even when past history suggests otherwise, because you might just find yourself pleasantly surprised by the actions of people like your dumb little brother, who maybe isn't so dumb after all.

After a lunch consisting of Fiona quizzing my mother about the number of childhood friends and girlfriends I had ("I remember a neighbor girl named Julie Quint," Mom told her, which got Fi excited until I reminded my mother that the Quints moved while I was still in preschool, and then she mentioned three friends, including Andre, who were currently guests of the state of Florida), I decided to wait until after we ordered dessert to bring up the uninvited appearance of Davey Harris in my life, or at least in the Target I frequent.

"Ma," I said, "I can't stress this enough. You can't keep telling people your son the spy is home."

"I don't see why not," she said, "no one believes me, anyway."

"There's a reason I didn't tell you what I was doing all those years. You've seen enough now to know that it's not a thing to play with. So if someone asks what I do for a living, just tell them I'm in sales. Retail. Import. Export."

"I hate to lie, Michael," she said.

"Since when?"

"Since always."

"Well, then, just pretend. You don't have a sudden moral opposition to pretending, do you?"

"You used to love pretending."

"When you do it for a living," I said, "it becomes a little less fun. Just, please, avoid the subject of what I do. Or did. We'll all be safer."

A sprightly dressed waiter dropped off a plate of chocolate cake for my mother, another mudslide for Fi and a squirt of frozen yogurt for me. For a time, we ate in silence. It felt nice. I hoped I'd essentially put a cap on the issue and we could all live our lives in perfect happiness for another thirty minutes, or at least the amount of time it took me to meet up with Sam and find out what job he'd conscripted me into.

"Did he play dress-up?" Fi asked my mother.

"Here we go," I said.

"There was a time when he was twelve that he pretended for a week to have a broken leg," Ma said. "Limped everywhere he went."

"You made me do that," I said.

"How could I make you pretend to have a broken leg? That's just crazy, Michael."

"Well, Ma, as I recall, you ended up getting the TG&Y to give you a couple hundred bucks in store credit, since you claimed one of their shopping carts malfunctioned and ran me over."

My mother gets a nice blush of red in her face when she's angry. At that moment, she looked like an apple. "That's asinine," she said, but there wasn't much behind it, and she immediately began shoveling cake into her mouth.

"And didn't Nate 'pretend' to have a broken wrist, too?"

"You know, Michael, I was just trying to do my best to raise you two. If my methods were unconventional, I'm sorry."

"Unconventional? You had my leg put into a cast."

"And all of your friends signed it," she said. "It was wonderful for your self-confidence."

"Didn't we just determine that I didn't have any friends, Ma?" I said.

"I'm going outside to smoke a cigarette." My mother stood up, grabbed her purse and tucked her vase in the crook of her arm. "You can ruin someone else's Mother's Day if you like, but you're not going to ruin mine."

I leaned back in my chair and finished off my frozen yogurt, aware that Fiona was glaring at me. "What?" I said, finally.

"You're just going to let her stand out there?"

"She put my leg in a cast, Fi," I said.

"When you were twelve."

"Exactly."

Fi grabbed my elbow. Hard. "And I could put your arm in one now," she said.

Sometimes Fiona's violent streak is cute. Sometimes it's just violent. This was the latter. "Fine," I said, but by the time I got outside, Ma was already gone. And I hadn't even had the chance to give her the Crock-Pot and toaster oven yet.

3

One of the benefits of covert ops is that money is never an issue. If you're having dinner with Chadian Aozou rebel leaders in Southern Libya and you set your Visa down, there's never any concern that you won't have enough room on your card to cover the bill. If you must purchase a decommissioned Soviet-era tank to ease tensions among opposing warlords in the Sudan, there's never a call to your bank to check your credit rating. If you need to get your hands on a million dollars to pay off someone and that someone isn't going to turn around and bomb U.S. interests, you don't have to wait five business days for the funds to clear your bank.

When you've been burned and you have to worry about the price of detergent and the sudden rise in dairy costs affecting your yogurt consumption, making sure you have a steady cash stream takes on new importance.

Something Sam knows all too well, which is

why I wasn't exactly bamboozled when he told me about the client he'd met with earlier in the day.

"Thing of it is, Mike," he said, "this is the kind of job I literally could do on my own without a problem, but I've been reading the newspapers lately and I'm not afraid to say that, for those working freelance, the outlook is pretty bleak."

"Funny," I said, "I didn't see any stories in the *Herald* detailing the plight of the out of work spy."

We'd been sitting on the Carlito's patio for a little more than twenty minutes, largely making idle chatter, which is how Sam warms up before breaking bad news to me. So we'd already covered my shopping adventure at Target, the exploding ship and my exploding mother, which brought us to the job at hand. There was a thin manila file on the table that Sam hadn't mentioned yet.

"Well, you gotta read between the lines," Sam said. "You can't trust that the media is going to say the exact truth. Little propaganda here, little propaganda there, keeps people on an even keel. Price of gas, for instance. Prime indicator of tough financial times ahead in the industry, my friend. Even your average drug smuggler or arms guy is going to take a long look at the ledger before he decides to make the Atlantic run with a bunch of cargo."

"I get it, Sam," I said.

"I'm just saying, you never know where your next dollar might come from."

This already sounded bad. "But you're going to tell me, aren't you?"

Sam plucked an oyster from the bowl in front of him and then took a long sip from a bottle of Stella. "How do you feel about boats?"

"That depends, Sam. Are they blowing up?"

"Of course not," Sam said.

"Because I saw a really nice yacht turned into slivers today and I don't have a pressing desire to be involved in that sort of thing."

"Thing of it is," Sam said, "a friend referred me to a gentleman in the Italian yacht industry who has a rather significant problem."

"The Italian yacht industry?"

"Yes," Sam said.

"Didn't I tell you that I wasn't interested in Mob business?"

"This isn't the Mob," Sam said, but he said it in such a way that I sensed there was some semantic interpretation at work.

"I have no desire to enter into some squabble with Cosa Nostra," I said. "The Outfit. Cosca. The Family. Whatever word you want to use. You're talking about two hundred years of pissed-off people. They are not my problem."

"It's not that yacht industry," Sam said.

"No?"

"Not specifically."

"What yacht industry do you think I'm speaking of?"

Sam pondered this for a moment. "The one that takes place at the shipyards. Right?"

"Who is the friend?" I asked. This was important. Many of Sam's friends in the past were actually people who were friends with his former girlfriend Veronica, which meant they had some problem that could only be solved to my near peril. Other friends of his were people who lived in that nebulous territory between smuggler and outright pirate, and who'd found themselves in situations requiring backup. And others still were people who bought him drinks when he was low on cash and learned his long and sordid history and figured he might be able to help them avoid violent exes, shylocks, bookies, unpleasant organized solicitors upon their businesses and other sundry unpleasant societal ills.

No one ever needed a cat rescued from a tree.

No one ever needed someone to give their son a stern talking-to about fireworks.

No one ever needed a guy to water their plants and watch their poodle, even.

"Maybe *friend* is a bit of a stretch," Sam said. "A guy I know from a thing I did in Latvia a few years ago—let's just say it was totally legal within the constructs of common treaties currently in place—has a small business venture whereby certain people come to him looking for help with projects that require sensitivity and care in the retrieval of certain products or persons. A former client of his contacted him today in relation to an event of a dangerous nature."

"So," I said, "a mercenary?"

"Essentially," Sam said.

"If he's so good," I said, "why did he need to come to you with things of a 'dangerous nature'?"

"This job is a little out of his area of expertise."

On the beach, people were playing volleyball, tossing Frisbees, applying suntan lotion. A bank of thick gray clouds lined the horizon, making me think that a storm might be coming, or if it were like any other Miami afternoon, they'd just sit out there all day as if to let everyone know that somewhere else people had it just slightly worse.

I sighed. It was better than speaking.

"And my friend isn't technically allowed in America," Sam said.

I sighed again. This one was meant to convey a sense of quiet resignation tinged with muddled anger.

"Now, Mikey," Sam said, "I wouldn't have agreed to take this job if it didn't seem like something you could do with your eyes closed. You wouldn't even need to take off your sunglasses."

"Where is this client?"

"He's staying at the Setai," Sam said.

The Setai is the most expensive hotel in South Beach. It's the kind of hotel you stay in when you want people to know that money means nothing to you, but not in the frugal sense. Odds are that if you're staying at the Setai, you don't have a Crock-Pot and a toaster oven in your trunk, you didn't have lunch at T.G.I. Friday's and your problems are not the kind that can be solved with your sunglasses on.

"Who is this person? One of the Medicis?"

Sam cleared his throat, "Gennaro Stefania." He waited, as if I might suddenly bolt from the table, or pass out, or have any response at all.

"That supposed to mean something to me?"

"At any time in the last ten years did you pick up a magazine with an actress or model on the cover?"

"No."

"*People*?"

"No."

"You are aware such magazines exist?"

"I am aware that I'm about thirty seconds from going home."

Sam slid the manila file folder toward me. I opened it and saw a photo of a man on the deck of a catamaran cutting through rough seas. There were other men surrounding him, but for reasons unknown their faces were pixelated. The man looked to be about forty, athletic, his arms long and sinewy with muscle, like a runner's. He was handsome in a regular way, which is to say he didn't look like a model, just your average alpha male: an angular face, deep-set green eyes, wavy brown hair.

I turned the page and saw a word that immediately made me close the file: Ottone.

The Ottones were a family made for tabloid journalism. They were nineteenth-century money that had migrated from land wealth in the Old World to the currency of luxury: the Lux, a two-seater sports car modeled after their Formula One racecars, which became quickly favored in the 1970s by men on their way to the disco and the women who loved them, in the '80s by would-be investment bankers and the women who held their cocaine and hair gel, in the '90s by midlife-crisis humans of all sexes who didn't realize they weren't driving Porches. In the twenty-first century, they sold their car line to Ford and began a full-throttle investment into opulence: clothing lines, jewelry, watches, fragrance, casino properties. They added their name to anything that connoted the good life, including Fashion Week in Milan, tennis tournaments and golf opens in Dubai, polo in England, open-wheel racing in Monte Carlo, nightclubs in New York and Los Angeles that attracted people who merely wanted to be near the kind of money they'd never earn. In a few years people would think *Ottone* was just another word, not a proper name.

And with all of that, of course, comes scandal. Mistresses, drug addictions, deaths—the sorts of things that happen to normal people all the time but that are heightened by a place in world society.

A place I was not interested in being a part of.

A place Gennaro Stefania was connected with by virtue of being married to Maria Ottone, which was a little like being married to the key to Fort Knox.

A place that invariably led to publicity. Not what a burned spy craves, ironically.

"Not interested," I said, and slid the file back to Sam.

"His family is in peril," Sam said. His voice was serious, but I could tell that he'd practiced that line. Peril wasn't a word that rolled off Sam's tongue.

"Isn't that the sort of thing that would be on the news by now?"

"It's complicated," Sam said.

"This is not something I can do with my sunglasses on, Sam, I can tell you that already."

"It'll be a piece of cake," Sam said, "trust me." He swallowed the last of his Stella and stood up.

"You going somewhere?"

"We're already late," Sam said. "You think you could call your brother and see if he could pick us up? Can't exactly pull up to the Setai in the Charger, you know? You mind?"

"I do mind," I said.

"He's a good kid," Sam said.

"He's not a kid, Sam," I said. "He's an actual adult. You really want him parked in front of that hotel while we meet with *your* client?"

Sam thought about that. "What's the worst that could happen?"

"That shouldn't be the baseline consideration," I said.

Sam pulled out his phone. "Let me see if I can get a buddy of mine to loan us something appropriate."

The difference between being wealthy and being rich isn't so much a question of dollars and cents as it is an understanding of levels. When you're rich, you might have a vacation house in Sun Valley or the Hamptons, might have a Bentley or two, might have a photo of yourself with the president on the wall of your office. Maybe you're a lawyer or a doctor, or you invented doubled-sided tape and thus have a net worth in the millions of dollars earned off your own hard work and expertise and invention.

You're rich.

When you're wealthy, you don't have a second home, you have a second island, the president or premier or king or violent despot is probably in your pocket (particularly in certain OPEC nations) and you probably don't have to worry about punching a clock, since the other key difference is that wealth perpetuates wealth generationally—so that men like petrochemical scions Mukesh and Anil Ambani don't need to create anything new whatsoever; they just need to wait for their parents to die, and even if they end up feuding and suing each other and breaking apart the companies they inherited, they still both end up being worth more than $40 billion each. Not a bad day's work, if you can get it.

You're wealthy.

The other option toward untold wealth, particularly if you don't want to work terribly hard for it, is age-old and difficult to ever understand completely: love. People have married for much less than a billion dollars, but in the case of Gennaro Stefania, most people figured it was the billions, not love, which led to his romance and eventual marriage to Maria Ottone a little more than a decade ago.

I was in the passenger's seat of Sam's buddy's car—a BMW that smelled like people had been having sex in it, regularly, and in all of the seats— reading through Gennaro's file again as we made our way to the Setai. I was trying to figure out why someone like him would need someone like me, but, more than that, why he might have needed someone like Sam's nebulous friend, particularly a nebulous friend who would provide such an extensive dossier, which detailed his life in familiar CIA-speak and description and detail.

"Your friend," I said. "What did he do for Gennaro before?"

"Security mostly," Sam said.

"Security like he protected him, or security like he hid bodies for him?"

"Security like he helped him out of a problem with some undesirables. It's on page six."

One thing I knew for certain was that marrying into the Ottone clan was no easy bargain, money or not. But especially not for someone like Gennaro, who wasn't exactly Italian royalty. He was the American-born son of Victor Stefania, who'd raced for the Ottone's Formula One team in the '60s and '70s and died in a fiery crash I remembered watching with my dad on ABC's *Wide World of Sports*. I could still hear Jim McKay announcing the race, the slow-motion replays of the car flipping over the grassy midfield of some foreign track before turning supernova. "That's the agony of defeat," my dad said then, which says a lot about Dad.

The dossier said Gennaro lived in America through college, moved to Italy after the death of his mother from cancer and married into the Ottone clan a decade ago amid persistent rumors that it was some kind of reparation for his father's service, but, at least looking at the photos of him with Maria and their young daughter, things seemed bucolic, rumor and gossip aside. He'd inherited his father's love of speed, but he preferred his work on the water—a lot less chance for fireballs, that afternoon's activities notwithstanding—and was now the helmsman for Ottone's yacht racing team, the *Pax Bellicosa*, which was in Miami to take part in the Hurricane Cup.

Yacht racing is one of those sports that the average American doesn't care about because the average American is landlocked. Even still, the idea of taking part in a regatta probably conjures images of men in navy blue sport coats calling each other *old chap* and *sport* and *chum* while skirting around buoys in the pleasant waters of the Atlantic, which certainly isn't as compelling as anabolic freaks slamming into each other for a hundred yards of contested territory, ten yards at a time.

The truth was that there was a lot of "old chap" this and "sport" that and "chum" tossed around New England, but on the world stage, yacht racing was big business and big entertainment, which meant, as with all things big, that there was a criminal element. I didn't think that yacht blowing up beneath the causeway this afternoon was a faulty wiring issue, certainly. There were also million-dollar parties, secondary events like fashion shows and car expos and haute cuisine displays. And gambling, though not of the legal variety. These teams, like Gennaro's, were owned by people who threw money around like confetti. Where there's money, there's desire for more, and desire makes people blind. Blind people stumble into stupid things, like stickups, heists and good old-fashioned extortion, all in the name of sport.

Nevertheless, Gennaro seemed normal enough, which probably meant he was completely corrupt.

I flipped to page six.

"Oh, this is surprising," I said.

"I'm not convinced it's going to be a problem," Sam said, but he might as well have said that he didn't think he'd ever want to drink another beer. Some lies are well-meaning. Others are just lies.

There was a picture of Gennaro with Christopher Bonaventura, head of one of the largest international crime families. Allegedly. It was taken from a distance of several hundred yards and captured the two of them walking along a rocky jetty. The photo was likely snapped from a dinghy somewhere in the Adriatic. "What is this, Sam?"

"They're old friends," Sam said. "There was a question of impropriety that arose from the friendship. My friend smoothed it out."

"What kind of impropriety?"

"There was some thought Gennaro had debts he wasn't informing his family about."

"Gambling?"

"Drugs. Bonaventura moves a lot of H. Seeing the two of them together raised suspicions. Especially since they weren't exactly meeting in front of Starbucks."

"Who was tailing him?"

"Don't know. Probably Bonaventura's own guys."

"And your friend smoothed it out how?"

Sam shifted in his seat. It was his one tell. Sometimes he just can't sit with things. "He convinced

Mr. Bonaventura that he was no longer friends with Gennaro."

"You couldn't have told me this when we were still at the Carlito?"

"Gennaro doesn't believe his situation is related to this. Frankly, Mikey, I'm inclined to believe the kid."

I flipped back through the dossier. "He's almost forty."

"He's very innocent," Sam said. "You'll want to protect him when you see him."

"I'll probably want to shake him until he passes out."

Up ahead, the Setai shimmered in the fading sun. The hotel was a strange and entirely appropriate nexus between the past and the present, as if Art Deco had gone on a long, hot date with Asian design aesthetics. Look one way, you were in Miami in 1933. Look the other, and it was Hong Kong fifteen minutes ago. Half of the hotel was the old Dempsey-Vanderbilt, which first entertained the rich and notorious eighty years ago; the other half was a forty-story tower that was a second home to any celebrity with a single name.

"You going to tell me who your friend is?" I asked. It wasn't important on a personal level, just that Sam's patented avoidance of the subject made me curious and also indicated to me that our new friend Gennaro probably had issues beyond the dossier.

"A guy named Jimenez. That's all I can say."

"CIA?"

"For a time."

"NSA?"

"Just an old friend, Mikey. He assures me Gennaro is fine and totally on the level. And rich, Mikey. Big money here. The kind where you won't have to work for months afterward and can just focus on figuring out your burn notice."

"Just the vacation I've been hoping for," I said.

We pulled up to the hotel and were met by a valet dressed in an all-brown Nehru outfit. He took Sam's keys without muttering a single word or looking directly at either one of us before speeding off. Indifference was the new politeness.

"Not exactly the Motel 6 here," Sam said.

"You get what you pay for," I said.

"But do they leave the lights on for you?"

"I'm going to guess that they do," I said.

"My money, all you really need in a hotel is a bed, a bar and a pool."

"Well," I said, "good thing it's not your money."

Inside, the Setai was oddly quiet. I'd grown so accustomed to every hotel in South Beach being an excuse for a nightclub to have a roof that I'd forgotten elegance still existed. The lobby began as a narrow expanse that widened out across the back of the hotel, so that you got the sense you were looking into the hotel through a Panavision camera, your eyes taking in each new design detail as you moved across the brushed travertine floor. Throughout the space were vases of white roses atop nested tables beside matte bronze sofas that looked comfortable enough to sleep on, but which not a soul was sitting on. The muted glow of candles created fanciful shadows on the walls, which were also an understated bronze highlighted by long black draping and grand pieces of oval-shaped marble.

At the far end of the lobby was a single stomach-high reception desk made of brushed steel and inlaid squares of marble and wood. A man and a woman stood behind the counter. Both wore those odd Nehru outfits, and as we neared them en route to the elevators their faces turned downcast.

"You know what I miss?" Sam said.

"I dunno, Sam. The Cold War?"

"Used to be you walked into a hotel, it didn't feel like you were somehow annoying the employees. This place, it's pretty, but it's not Howard Johnson's."

The last time the two of us spent a substantial amount of time in a high-rise hotel in the service of the superrich, Sam ended up taking out most of the fifth floor of the Hotel Oro. I had the sense that doing the same here would not be met with indifference. The Hotel Oro was owned by Russians of dubious intent. The Setai was owned by the GHM chain, the difference being the hotel chain would be more likely to chase you to the ends of the planet with a passel of lawyers. I'll take Russians of dubious intent any day over lawyers. So, I made it a point to give the dour humans behind the reservations desk a nice smile as we passed.

Nothing. Not even a wave.

We took the elevators up to the fortieth floor, where they opened to the penthouse level. I expected to be greeted by some tough guys in suits, because that's normally what you find at the entrance to a penthouse suite, but the hallway was empty save for the marble floor and the impressionist paintings on the wall alongside archival photos of the hotel in its Prohibition past.

"How much you suppose a room up here costs?" Sam said.

"Twenty grand," I said.

"You think that includes breakfast?"

"I'm going to say no," I said.

"Howard Johnson's, you get a buffet breakfast and a room for a C-note."

"It's a cruel world." I knocked on the door. I thought maybe when it opened I'd finally get to see my tough guys in suits, but instead Gennaro Stefania himself opened the door. He wore tan shorts, a polo shirt with the Ottone logo on the breast and no shoes. He was tanned and healthy-looking from a distance, but up close you could see that his eyes were red and puffy. I didn't think it was from lack of sleep.

"You must be Michael Westen," he said.

"We all must be someone," I said. We shook hands, but there wasn't much there. It was like shaking a straw man. You could tell he was a fine-tuned athlete, but there was a lot being sapped out of him.

"Come in," he said, and stepped out of the way for Sam and me to pass. "Let me give you the tour, for what it's worth."

We stepped into the penthouse and Gennaro took us through room by room, and only then did I realize what being part of the Ottone family meant: there were two living rooms in the penthouse, a separate music room that featured a Steinway piano, and at least 10,000 square feet, which was needed since there were four bedrooms, four baths replete with Jacuzzis, even quarters for a butler. There was also a full bar with flat screen televisions and a stocked cigar humidor.

"You mind?" Sam said to Gennaro. Surprisingly, he was pointing to the humidor and not the five bottles of Macallan 30 year or the two dozen Samuel Adams Utopia blend beers.

"Help yourself," Gennaro said. "It's all paid for."

That's the wrong thing to say to Sam, who took one Cuban to smoke and grabbed a few more for a rainy day. Another couple for the sunny days, too.

"Just like Howard Johnsons," I said.

The penthouse was surrounded by a wraparound terrace that featured an eternity pool and another hot tub, as if the four inside weren't enough.

But the curious thing was that Gennaro was all alone.

"Nice place," I said.

"It's too much," Gennaro said. "It's all too much."

"You could rent the bathrooms out by the hour," Sam said. He was trying to be funny, maybe make Gennaro crack at least the smallest smile, but I could tell he was in no mood.

"Why don't we sit down," I said and Gennaro just nodded, but didn't really move. It was as if he was in a trance and needed someone to give him even the most rudimentary cues so he'd know what to do with himself. So I said, "Why don't we sit down on one of the nine sofas?"

Gennaro nodded again and made his way toward an L-shaped taupe sofa that was positioned so that it faced out toward the sea. He dropped into the corner of the L, like he was being punished, and just stared out the window. I pulled a chair up and sat across from him and motioned for Sam to join me, which meant he had to pull himself away from the Utopias, which he'd just discovered.

"So," I said, once Sam was beside me, "tell me your problem."

Gennaro reached into his pocket, pulled out an

iPhone and handed it to me. "Two days ago," Gennaro said, "I received that message in my e-mail."

The e-mail contained a link to a Web site, which when opened began running a surveillance video of Maria Ottone and her young daughter, Liz. For about twenty seconds, it just watched them sleeping in what looked to be a stateroom on a boat. It then cut to a shot of them eating lunch, another of them sunning themselves on the deck, their daughter playing with a Barbie, and again it cut to a shot of Maria showering, the focus getting closer and closer on Maria's face until you could see the small freckles along her jawline, the fine skin on her cheekbones, the flick of her tongue when a long piece of her hair found the corner of her mouth. It then began running other clips, just a few seconds of the mundane, enough to let whomever was watching know that they were observing Maria and Liz at every single moment.

"Where is your wife?" I said. The images were still flitting past. There was no sound on the video. Just the images in silence, which somehow made them all the more disturbing.

"She's on a boat in the middle of the Atlantic," he said.

"Whose boat?"

"Her boat. Our boat. One of the family's boats. She's on her way from Italy to here. She hates to fly."

"When was the last time you spoke to her?"

"Thirty minutes ago."

"And she's fine?"

"Of course," he said. "I've done everything they've asked." His eyes were getting red again.

Crying women make me uncomfortable. Crying children make me feel self-conscious. Crying men make me want to shower with my clothes on.

"How did they contact you?"

"Two, three minutes after I logged onto the Web site, the phone began ringing. I didn't pick it up right away, because I didn't know what I was looking at. I mean, that's my wife. That's my daughter. I couldn't put it together."

"I understand," I said.

"So it could have been five, ten minutes later that I finally picked up. I don't know how many times they called."

"Was it a man or a woman on the phone?"

"I couldn't tell," he said. "The voice sounded strange. Like that guy in the wheelchair."

"Ironside?" Sam said.

"The scientist. The smart guy."

"Stephen Hawking?" I said.

"Like that. Like it was coming through a computer."

It used to be that only the most sophisticated governments had access to spy technology, but today anyone with a decent laptop and access to an Office Max can employ entry-level spy craft.

The entire Cuban Missile Crisis could have been averted today using Google. Any twelve-year-old can download voice-changing software for free on the Internet. The difference now is not the technology, but about how savvy you are in using it.

"Hold that thought," I said to Gennaro. I turned to Sam. "You trace this Web site?"

"It's a pro job," Sam said. "Registered through a company in Qatar to Neil Diamond."

"He'll be easy to find."

"His Web site says he's doing ten sold-out nights in Las Vegas. I could be there in five hours, grab him during 'Sweet Caroline.'"

"He might be a patsy. What else?"

"They used open-source software on the design, so there's no technology fingerprint on it. It's a secure site, so only following the embedded link here will get you to it. The video is on a continuous loop. Gene here says they've been adding new stuff to it every day."

"Any way to hack into the code and see who else is viewing it? Get an IP number or a country code? Anything?"

"I already poked around, but the encryption is first-rate," Sam said. "We're working with experts here."

"You have someone you could show it to?" I asked. Sam always has someone he can show things to. He collects people and favors like lint.

"I'll talk to a buddy of mine."

I turned back to Gennaro. "Okay," I said. "How much do they want?"

"Nothing."

"Nothing?"

"They said if I didn't lose the Hurricane Cup, they'd kill Maria and Liz."

4

Provided you're not a serial killer, sociopath or pederast, if you're in the business of kidnapping people, it's usually for one of three reasons:

You want money.

You have political, religious and/or world-domination plans.

You are out for revenge.

In Mexico, kidnappings are up 30 percent since the drug dealers have had a loss of revenue recently because of a saturated market, so they've started to diversify into other business opportunities. The advantage of kidnapping someone is that there's very little competition. You want someone, you just take them.

The only legit reason you'd fix a sporting event would be for monetary gain—not even Raiders fans would kidnap a woman and a child to ensure victory, so it didn't stand to reason that the millionaires who wagered on the yacht races would be willing to be criminally fervent.

You kidnap a member of the Ottone family, you want *something*, even if you say you want *nothing*.

"Tell me exactly what they said," I said to Gennaro.

"They told me that they had my wife and daughter, that they were on the boat with them, watching them, and that if I followed the rules, nothing would happen. If I pulled out of the race, or won it, they'd kill them both. All I had to do was lose the Hurricane Cup and no one would be the wiser."

"So then you should lose the Hurricane Cup," I said. "And you should put your expatriate tax dollars to work and call the FBI."

"It's not that simple," Gennaro said. He got up from the sofa abruptly, opened the sliding glass door and stepped out to the terrace, where he stood with his back to Sam and me while he looked out over the ocean. His hair was whipped by swirling winds—on the fortieth floor, you can't really expect it all to be perfect, can you?—and I could also see that his polo shirt was rippling against his skin. It just didn't look all that pleasant out there. So I didn't get up.

"You gonna go out there, Mikey?"

"He's the second person to get up from me in the middle of a conversation today."

"Sounds like your mother had good reason," Sam said.

"Really?"

"You know what they say in the SEALs," Sam said. "A cup of sugar is easier to swallow than a cup of anthrax."

"I don't recall hearing that."

"Maybe it was a cup of dimethylmercury. Anyway, sentiment here is the rule of the day."

"I shouldn't have to interrogate our own clients, Sam."

"Rich people aren't like you and me, Mikey. They like to be served. Makes them remember what it was like having serfs."

"Fine," I said. "But if he gets dramatic on me again, I'm leaving." Sam and I walked outside and stood on either side of Gennaro, in case he decided to jump, or in case I decided to throw him off. He turned and looked at us both with what could only be described as dispassion, as if we were somehow ruining his moment.

"Gene, why don't you tell Mikey about your mitigating circumstances?"

Mitigating circumstances never sounded like good news. Invariably, it was the sort of thing that meant I was going to get shot at.

"You have to understand that there is a tremendous amount of pressure related to being the son of Victor Stefania," Gennaro said.

"I can appreciate that," I said.

"It might not be the case here in America, but he was part of the world culture. People feel like he was part of *them*, not just a person they saw racing on television. I saw my father die, but so did fifty million other people. Do you know what that's like?"

"No." I didn't bother to tell him that I was one of those fifty million.

"And there's another level when you've married into the Ottone family. It's not like you marry a girl you met in a bar or went to college with. It's . . . international. It's . . . generational. There are family problems that date to before the American Revolution."

I didn't like where this was headed. But I let Gennaro continue on, because sometimes I like to think that people will flip the page and I won't be reading the book I thought I was reading. Usually, they flip the page and it turns out that things are topsy-turvy and I'm in the middle of a pop-up book filled with dragons and moats and hobbits. I was hoping this would be something like a Victorian romance.

"Being on a team owned by the family isn't like being on a team where you're just the employee. You probably don't have context for this, but I'm the only man in the family who has amounted to anything."

"I have some context for that," I said.

"And I'm not even really family. Not in some of their eyes. I'm Maria's husband and I'm Liz's father, but I'm not an Ottone. And I'm not a hundred percent Italian. My mother was from California, just a mutt like everyone else out there. With Maria, it doesn't matter. We are bedrock. And it's not just because of Liz. And it's not all that gossip shit you read. Maria truly is the love of my life. But it's her family. Her mother. Her stepfather, really."

In the dossier, it said Maria's stepfather was Nicholas Dinino. He married Maria's mother five years ago after the death of her husband, the family's patriarch and the holder of the royal lineage, or at least the Ottone lineage. Dinino owned the yacht team, which made him Gennaro's father-in-law and de facto boss, too. Not an easy arrangement.

"I get it. You're living in a Crock-Pot." At some point, I thought, I needed to see my mother. . . .

"Like you wouldn't believe."

"Tell me something, Gennaro, were you on drugs?"

"No, no, never."

"Then what was going on with you and Christopher Bonaventura?"

"I've known him since I was twelve. We went to boarding school together in Connecticut. His father and my father used to go to Studio 54 together. It was like that, you know? We have a lot of similar issues related to our extended families. He was just someone I could turn to. That's all."

I didn't believe Gennaro. Not exactly. I trusted that they were friends, but somehow this situation with his wife was tied to his friendship. Or at least his refusal to go to the authorities was. I felt Gennaro dancing around the issue, and if there's one thing I find more disturbing than a man crying in front of me, it's a man dancing in front of me. Makes me nervous. Makes me feel like I'll be asked to do some sort of boot-scoot boogie, and that wasn't happening.

"Tell me you're not already throwing races, Gennaro."

"I'm not," he said. Before I could even exhale with relief, he said, "But I think they're being fixed behind me. The *Pax Bellicosa* should not be winning as we are. Not with me as the helmsman."

"You *think*?" I looked at Sam. He was puffing on his Cuban and attempting to look absolutely engrossed by the moon.

"Look," Gennaro said, "this hasn't been the best year for me, for my family, so I called in a favor a few months ago. One favor. That was it. Just to get me pointed in the right direction. Take me out of the cooker."

"Let me guess. You put in a call to Christopher Bonaventura."

"One race. That was it. Just asked him to help me get in position to place. I didn't even have to win."

"Was this before or after he was warned away from you?"

"After."

"Stay right here," I said to Gennaro, and gave him a big, big smile, the kind I normally reserve for angry mullahs preparing to torture me, and pulled Sam away from the terrace and back inside. "Your friend Jimenez. He fail to mention this to you?"

"This is all news to me."

"You recognize that this isn't an easy job, correct?"

"I'm beginning to sense that it might be more intricate than first was apparent. New intel. All that. But what can you do? I don't see anyone flying around Miami with a cape on these days."

I pointed at Sam. I didn't have words to speak. So I just kept pointing until I felt calm enough to go back outside and speak to Gennaro. "So I understand," I said when I got back to the terrace. "The mafia has fixed races so that you win, is that correct?"

"No." He was starting to look green. That's what happens to a guy when he realizes he's spent all day digging the grave his wife and child could be buried in.

I said, "I am not here to judge you. I am here to help you. If you lie to me, there's nothing I can do. I walk out this door and you and I never met."

Gennaro leaned over the balcony and exhaled hard. His shoulders slumped, and I could see the muscles in his jaw working. It wasn't pride that was keeping him from giving the whole story—it

was shame. Sam stepped back outside, but I gave
him a little wave to let him know I wanted Gennaro to myself for a minute, which Sam took to
mean now would be a good time to stretch out on
one of the two-dozen chaise lounges with his Cuban and a bottle of Utopia. You get the chance to
drink a hundred-dollar bottle of beer, I guess you
take it.

"This hotel used to be owned by Jack
Dempsey," I said. "Did you know that?"

Gennaro looked up at me, eyebrows raised, like
he wasn't sure where I was headed. "The boxer?"
he said.

"Yeah. Back in the 1930s it was called the
Dempsey-Vanderbilt. But it was just the small Art
Deco part down below," I said. I pointed over the
ledge, and Gennaro craned his head to get a look.
"When I was a kid, my dad brought me and my
brother, Nate, down here. Dempsey was signing
autographs and pretending to hit people. Putting
on a show, basically. By that point he didn't own
the hotel or anything. He was an old man from
history books, really. But here was a guy who,
back in the day, was considered the toughest man
alive. 1919, 1920, when you were heavyweight
champion of the world, it wasn't like now where
you fight once or twice a year; you fought all the
time. Plus, he was the kind of guy who'd fight
just for fun. Go into a bar. Call someone out. Even
after he retired, he kept fighting in exhibitions, just

to keep hitting people. Now, I'm not an athlete, so I don't know what that's like, that need to always be competing, but I'd guess that's pretty intoxicating?"

"Better than just about anything," Gennaro said.

"Thing of it is, you know what people remember most about Dempsey? What everyone wanted to talk to him about that day?"

Gennaro said he didn't know.

"One of his last fights, he got in the ring with a guy named Gene Tunney. There was a dispute about how much time the ref gave to Tunney after Dempsey knocked him down, and how little time was given to Dempsey when Tunney knocked him down. No one said the fix was in, but that hint of impropriety, it followed Dempsey around for the rest of his life. He never knew if he really won, or if he really lost. So there he was, sitting downstairs behind a table covered in bunting, talking about a fight that took place fifty years earlier. And you could just see it on him. The doubt. Like he wanted to fight the fight all over again."

I paused to let what I'd said to Gennaro sink into his skin. That I didn't know anything about Gennaro prior to that day didn't change the fact that, to a segment of society, he was considered one of the world's finest athletes, if helmsmen can be considered athletes. I suppose if NASCAR drivers and jockeys are classified as such, competitive yacht racers probably have equal claim to the designation.

"Christopher just told me he'd give me a better chance not to lose, that's all," he said. "I still had to race to win. I wanted my skill and my boat to win out at the end, not have it be something where I just coasted in."

"Do you even hear yourself?" I said. "This is your wife and child we're talking about. This is what you're going to stand on when your wife and child are shark bait?"

"He narrowed the field with his influence," Gennaro said. "The end game was easier to manage. That's all. But he's still doing it. I know."

"How?"

Gennaro squinted up at the darkening night sky. Clouds had rolled in and the air was thick with humidity, the moon and the stars obscured in gray, but the swirling winds atop the Setai made everything feel tinged with violence. "I'm not Jack Dempsey," he said.

"Then you call Bonaventura and you tell him to stop. You tell him that you need to race on your own."

"I can't just call him and tell him to stop."

"Sure you can. Same way you told him to start."

"I throw a race and then go to the FBI, you think Christopher would just let me walk away from that? How long before they'd be cornering Christopher? I make that call and I'm asking for trouble from Christopher that our friendship won't save. Maria, Liz, me, the whole family. Christopher won't care. He's made that clear enough."

When you go into business with the mafia, it's important to understand their organizational values and business model. Just like McDonald's, they are all about conceptualizing a franchise and then re-creating the concept over and over again, so that people get comfortable knowing that if they're in Pensacola or Paris or Prague, they can say "Big Mac, large fries and a Coke," and be fairly certain what they'll be getting back. You see that yellow M, Ronald McDonald and a bunch of severely underpaid employees and you feel relatively safe. With the mafia, the same principles are in place. You see a person like Christopher Bonaventura, you expect that he'll be able to "influence" a boat race in such a way that you have a better chance of winning. Trouble is the mafia isn't concerned with "better chances." They want an assured decision. Just like you don't want to order a Big Mac and get a lamb shank, the mafia wants to know that if they fix something, they'll see a return on their investment without fail.

It's called *organized crime* for a reason. When the mafia is run correctly, it can be as highly functional as a Fortune 500 company, with every aspect controlled and proctored and studied. The difference is that the mafia typically only ruins a few lives.

Christopher Bonaventura was suspected of ordering the murder of his father and his older brother. Killing Gennaro Stefania and half of the Ottone family wouldn't be fun, or without publicity, but if you're Christopher Bonaventura, bad publicity is the least of your concerns.

What was clear, however, was that he wasn't the person who'd surreptitiously kidnapped Maria and Liz. There was nothing working to his advantage from the act, and kidnapping simply wasn't mafia style, at least not one this intricate, where the people who've been kidnapped—and probably most of the crew of the boat—had no idea they were actually being held captive. If Christopher Bonaventura was responsible, Gennaro wouldn't have received a link to a secure Web site; he'd have received his daughter's Achilles tendon.

But if he was in Gennaro's life, there was a good reason to believe that he'd be lingering on the periphery of this all.

"When is the race?"

"It starts in two days," Gennaro said.

"Starts?"

"It takes a day, sometimes longer, to get to Bermuda."

"Bermuda?"

"We go from Miami to Nassau."

"Sam?" I said. Gennaro and I were still at the terrace, looking toward the sea. Toward Nassau. Toward the Bahamas.

"Yeah, Mikey," he said from behind me. His voice sounded a little husky, like maybe he'd closed his eyes while enjoying his contraband cigar and his bottle of the most expensive beer produced in the United States. Like he wasn't paying attention in the least, just enjoying the twenty-thousand-dollar-a-night view. Like he already knew how all of this was going to shake out.

"Seems Gennaro's race is going to take him out of Miami," I said. "Out of American waters entirely. All the way to Nassau. You ever been to Nassau, Sam?"

"Did a job there in 'ninety-two. Rumor was Carlos the Jackal was there taking a powder. Ended up totally erroneous. Splendid beaches, Mikey. You'd love it there."

"Unfortunately," I said, "I won't be going to the Bahamas, will I?"

"Oh, right, right," Sam said. He sat up. Rubbed at his eyes a little. Took a puff. Took a swallow. Like he didn't realize the high likelihood of a Coast Guard gunship waiting for me if I strayed too far from Miami. Or just the gun. "Well, if it turns out we can't solve Gene's problem before the race, I'll make the trip, Mikey." He looked at Gennaro, who, I could tell, didn't really like being called Gene in the least. "It's going to be no problem, Genie. Mike and I will solve this intricate riddle."

The riddle was a significant one. Whoever had

set up the surveillance on Maria and Liz knew
they could ask for a million dollars, or five million
dollars, or a bag of diamonds, and the Ottone
family would have no problem supplying the
demand. Money would mean nothing to them.
When Frank Sinatra Jr. was kidnapped by Barry
Keenan and his hapless pals, it wasn't because
Keenan loved "My Way." He was broke and
needed money to live on. In Colombia, where kidnapping is the lone growth industry in a sagging
economy, where they could practically put up
Chamber of Commerce billboards that say MORE
THAN THREE THOUSAND RANSOM KIDNAPPINGS
THIS YEAR! and no one would blush, since it's the
best investment opportunity in the country.

Most people don't just stumble into an abduc-
tion. If you kidnap someone, you usually have to
be willing to kill that person, and if you're willing
to kill someone—in this case, a woman and a
child—that means you're desperate. Barry Keenan
wasn't desperate, he was stupid, and when you're
stupid, you involve more stupid people in your
employ and eventually someone breaks, their mo-
rality gets the better of them, and the plot all falls
apart, as it did with Sinatra Jr. The Colombians
and Mexicans are desperate and engaged; a dangerous combination, but one that takes savvy. The
Colombian model involves in-depth knowledge of
the people you're pressuring, which made Gennaro's issue all the more curious. Whoever was on

the boat, whoever had contacted Gennaro, whoever needed him to lose, knew he couldn't go to the authorities, knew somewhere, somehow, that Gennaro had dirt on him that could get his wife and child and himself killed without any secondary exertion at all.

Intimate.

Elegant.

Flawless.

"This is going to be a costly mission," Sam said, as if he'd been listening in to my thought process, though more likely he was just thinking about how much he was enjoying the fruits of the mission thus far and wouldn't mind daily update meetings in the suite. "With the kind of intel we'll be reconning, this will require an absolute DEF-CON Level X-Ray Attachment, right, Mikey?"

Sometimes it's hard to remember that Sam used to be an actual Navy SEAL.

"I can pay whatever you need," Gennaro said. "That's not a concern."

I told Gennaro I'd need the names of everyone on the boat with his wife, the names of everyone who sailed with him on the *Pax Bellicosa* and a simple understanding that from now on, he answered to only one person.

Me.

"We need to make this problem disappear before you ever get on your yacht," I said. "Eliminate any possibility of problems, and make sure your wife and daughter are safe. When will they be in American waters?"

"Race day," he said. "Maria gets nervous when I race, so they'll be right outside Government Cut. She always says if she has to wait for me at the end, she won't have any nails left. But if she can see me stream past, when everyone is even, it's easier. I've never understood it. It sounds crazy, doesn't it?"

"No," I said. "Sounds like she just wants to see you perform. You watch the beginning of a two-day race, it's just the sport, not the competition."

"Maybe you're right," he said.

"She probably doesn't care if you win or lose, Gennaro," I said. "And neither does your father."

Gennaro reached out and shook my hand, and this time it felt like there was an actual body behind the hand.

"I trust you," Gennaro said.

"I'm going to get your wife and child off that boat alive."

"I know. I do."

"Good. Now you tell me something so I know I can trust you: Got any idea who might have blown up that million-dollar yacht this afternoon?" Gennaro nodded once, very slowly. It was enough. "Let me guess. It helped your end game?"

"This isn't the life I wanted," he said.

"Who has that, exactly?" I said.

"My wife," he said. "My daughter."

"Then we'll keep it that way."

We left Gennaro out on the terrace and made our way back to the elevator. Two days wasn't much time, but then kidnappers don't generally work with your schedule. Once you have the ability to manipulate time, you have the ability to manipulate emotion, which meant that we'd need to have an idea who the players were long before Gennaro took to the water.

"So," I said to Sam after we stepped into the elevator, "did you forget the part about the Bahamas?"

"I must have."

"And the part with the fixed races?"

"Took me by surprise."

"Because I asked you about that and, as I recall, you said it was impossible."

"It's hard to keep up with technology," Sam said. "Ten, fifteen years ago, you told people they could watch a movie on their telephone they would have sent you to an asylum. It's a crazy world, Mikey. Ever changing."

We rode the rest of the way down in silence, partially because I was waiting for Sam to start explaining to me why he hadn't told me all of the facts he certainly knew outside the sudden advent of great new technological advances in cheating, and partially because I think Sam was trying to figure out what his answers would be.

We made it back through the lobby, where we saw a woman who looked a lot like Madonna, and all the way out to the valet station. I was holding strong.

"Crap, Mikey," Sam said. "Are you gonna say something?"

"What would you like me to say?"

"I don't know. Something about this being a job for a Delta Force team? Maybe something snide about the amount of information I'd kept on the side. That sort of thing."

I had to give it to Sam. He knew me well. "When was the last time you tacked on the open sea, Sam?"

"It's been a few years. It all comes right back. You got nothing to worry about, Mikey."

"You're right," I said, and smiled, because when you can smile instead of scream, it's always a nice gambit.

"Once a SEAL," he said, though he didn't sound too confident, "always a SEAL. I'll pick up some deck shoes and we'll be good to go. Sign me up for the America's Cup." Sam turned and looked at the old Art Deco portion of the Setai and then looked back to me with a queer smile on his face. "That Jack Dempsey stuff with you and Nate and your dad. That really happen?"

"No," I said.

"Still," he said, "pretty good story."

"I wanted to go," I said, "but my dad wouldn't take me. I don't even know how old I was. Maybe seven or eight. Young, at any rate. Twenty years later, I'm making a dead drop in that one library in Namibia that had an English-language section and I find Dempsey's biography just sitting there, like it's been waiting for me all that time. I didn't have a Namibian library card, so I'm afraid I stole it."

"Namibia was a nice place," Sam said.

"If you like imploding tungsten mines."

"I find the smell of burning tungsten mines very relaxing."

"Not from the inside," I said.

The valet brought Sam's buddy's car around.

"What's different about my car?" Sam said.

"It's not actually your car," I said. "And it looks like they washed it."

Sam seemed duly impressed and compensated the valet for the cleaning by handing him five whole American dollars before we got in and drove off.

"Tell me something, Sam: Do you trust Gennaro?"

"Sure, Mikey," Sam said. "You saw the look on his face. I don't think you fake that kind of desperation."

Sam was probably right, but something was eating at me about the whole situation. A point that wasn't clear yet.

"Tomorrow, see if you can get some information on the Web site and any communications coming into his room."

"Sure. Buddy of mine can probably get the records for all the incoming calls. Might be interesting to see who's been calling Madonna, too."

"Let's just keep it focused on Gennaro," I said.

Sam agreed by grunting, so I expected to get a full report on Madonna's movements nonetheless.

Another thought occurred to me. "Do you happen to know anyone in town trying to sell plutonium?" I said.

"Not unless Bin Laden's on Spring Break," Sam said. "Why, you looking to take out Canada once and for all?"

"Fi said an old friend was in town," I said. "Just wanted to, you know, see if you'd heard anything."

"A few years from now, when you two are living behind a nice steel-enforced white picket fence at some secure location, you'll look back on this period of your life and laugh," Sam said. The funny thing was that he didn't say it with the slightest bit of irony.

5

When you're planning a clandestine operation, it's wise to keep your team small. People tend to notice fifteen men in body armor storming an embassy, so if you need to kill someone, steal something or map out a location for a future action, it's better to go alone if you can. Someone to watch your back and someone to guard your flank are helpful, but if you want to be sure a job gets done right, it's best to do it by yourself.

Less margin of error, which means less chance someone goes home in a coffin, and less chance that you'll be on Al Jazeera with a canvas bag over your head.

No one looks good with his head in a canvas bag.

The same rules apply to fixing a sporting event. There's nothing easy about fixing a match that involves the complicity of more than one person. Two men in a ring savagely beating each other is easy to control. Find the fighter with the Jell-O-like moral center and make your pitch. Give anyone enough money and it isn't difficult to convince them to stay on the ground after being hit in the face.

Try convincing nine men to throw a baseball game and you'll be lucky to get out alive. Same with hockey, basketball or football. You want to avoid angering men with bats or sticks or elbows sharpened on human skulls. As general policy, you also want to avoid situations where you're outsized by two or more feet and several hundred pounds by men who like to get hurt for fun.

So if you want to fix a team sport, you should try to shave points. This is easier than getting a team to win or lose and it requires only one person who plays a pivotal role to be desperate and stupid, versus an entire squad. So if you're Joe Quarterback or Jack Point Guard and you've found yourself in deep with the Russian Mafia, you might be inclined to throw an interception or brick a free throw or two to preserve the point spread (and your kneecaps) at the end of a game. And if you're lucky, your team still wins and you can sleep at night with only one Ambien instead of two.

In sports, however, there's also the inevitable entrance of luck. It doesn't matter if it's good or bad, just luck itself. A terrible shot somehow finds its mark. An intercepted football gets fumbled back into the hands of the offensive team. If you're a spy and have been sent to Azerbaijan to kill an arms dealer and miss when you shoot him, it's unlikely you'll be around to tell the story of how luck interceded, particularly if your head is in a canvas bag, with or without the rest of your body.

So if you're really invested in subterfuge as a profession, you want to find a sport that doesn't rely on any kind of points or any kind of luck. A sport that exists on an equal playing field, where wins and losses are calculated by human error, machinery and the unpredictable aspect of nature. Like horse racing. Betting on animals is stupid. They're animals. They don't know what they're doing. But at least the playing field is even, since none of the horses is any more sentient than the other. And because they are animals, they can't rat you out. Or NASCAR. The advent of the restrictor plate means that engine power became uniform in many of the races, or at least the races you'd want to fix, like Daytona and Talladega. Betting on cars is just as stupid as betting on animals, since they tend to break down, crash and then blow up and kill people, which frequently requires investigation. But cars don't speak, either, which means you can disable one without anyone ever knowing, particularly if you are at least somewhat adept with remote devices. And provided no one is immolated in the process, you might just get away with it, too.

Or boat racing. In a regatta, like the one the *Pax Bellicosa* was about to run in, all the yachts are precisely the same, Swan 45s, sleek racing yachts with towering sails totaling more than 1,400 feet of mainsail and jib. With the machinery uniform, you fix a race not by tweaking the system, but by altering—or failing to perform—the subtle duties of the people on the boat, none more so than the helmsman.

Gennaro's job.

Think of a helmsman like a quarterback, but one who not only knows how to throw a tight spiral and read defenses, but also has an intimate relationship with wind currents and retrograde velocity. The helmsman doesn't simply pilot the boat and direct the other members of the team; he interprets the elements.

The other men on the boat can effect change, too. It can be as simple as reacting a few moments late on an order, carrying more weight on your person than expected, or, if need be, falling overboard.

If you need to make a lot of money fast—and that means illegally—you want to avoid the ponies and cars, since both are bet on regularly without criminal involvement, and both are so deeply regulated that trying to muscle in to affect a race of any significance is simply not worth the time and effort. It would take less time to heist a casino.

But the international regatta world is different. The players—the people who own the yachts—are millionaires and billionaires, which means that

most of the fans are of a similar caste. Instead of a
league like the NFL, yacht racing is frequently
proctored, at least overseas, by the luxury corporations. Makers of watches, fine wines and cars ad-
vertise at these events to suggest a way of life. In
addition to the races, these corporations run a
week of events catering to every desire of the fan
base. This means fashion shows, wine tastings,
seminars where Warren Buffett comes in and talks
about how to fold money properly—things like
that.

According to that morning's *Miami Herald*, for
the next week the inhabitants of South Beach
would be worth collectively more than the GNP of
Honduras. It wasn't much of a surprise to me,
then, when I picked up Fiona and found her in a
more chipper mood than the day previous, particularly after I filled her in on the latest job I'd
found myself party to.

"You don't intend to pretend that you don't require payment again, do you?" she asked. We
were in the Charger heading toward my mother's
house. I thought bringing Fi with me on the drive
of shame back to my mother's house would make
it less awful. I didn't really want to go and fight
with my mother, but the longer I waited to drop
off her gifts, the more likely I was to take them
apart and use them for something else. Ever find
yourself imprisoned in your home and need to
make an IED? Turning a slow cooker into a bomb

takes only a few household cleaning items, a bit of foam from an old ice chest and, if you're looking to really hurt someone, a handful of paper clips, or, in a pinch, the zipper from your pants.

I also figured that if I had Fiona with me, two things might happen: I'd attempt to be more civil in the face of the now-vivid memories I had of my leg encased in plaster, and I'd be able to use her as an excuse to get out of recaulking the fireplace or cutting a cord of wood for the frigid spring months, or shoving my hand into the disposal again to fish out calcified animal fat.

"Sam was working on the financial end," I said.

"And to think your government used to trust you," she said.

"The job came through a contact of Sam's," I said.

"So now there's a finder's-keepers rule?"

"Whatever you need will be covered, Fi," I said. "But that doesn't mean you're coming out of this with your own catamaran. Just because these people have money doesn't mean anything."

I never liked taking money. It made this all feel like a job, like something I was now doing permanently versus doing to keep my skills up, or to bide time, or simply because it was the right thing to do. You're employed by the people when you're a spy, even if they aren't aware of it most of the time, and my feeling was that once I figured out my burn notice, I'd be paid back.

But, just the same, I have to eat. And Fi needs shoes and purses and that lipstick that makes her lips look irresistible, and I'd prefer she made money with me instead of selling guns or picking up jobs for bounty hunters and such.

Even if we weren't together as in *together*, life was still fundamentally more interesting with Fiona in the frame.

"I once owned a yacht, I'll have you know," Fi said.

"Owned?"

"*Possessed* might be a better word," she said.

"What does that mean?"

"It means for about a month I managed to live on one off the coast of Montenegro, fully staffed, even had a girl who came in and fluffed the pillows and a small boy who would come in at nightfall with a plate of cookies and chocolates."

"What happened?" I said.

"The owners came out of their comas."

"That happens," I said.

Fiona had the dossier from Sam's friend Jimenez and was flipping through it absently. Fi has always been more of a read-and-react kind of girl versus the type to do in-depth critical analysis, which means she's best on her feet with a gun or an M-19 grenade launcher or just her fists, using her experience as a guide instead of doctrine.

"He's cute," Fi said. I looked over and saw the photo of Gennaro with Bonaventura.

"Which one?"

"The gentleman in the fifteen-thousand-dollar suit."

"That's Christopher Bonaventura."

"I know."

"He's one of our problems."

"He doesn't look like much. He has a manicure in this photo. I've never liked a man who cared for his nails."

"I'm going to guess that he has a staff who digs the graves and dumps the people in them."

"Gennaro seems below his pay grade."

I explained to Fiona that when you get down to the working level of the yacht-racing business, after Rolex lays out their cash for their race and Ferrari theirs, much of the hard work, the swinging of hammers, the actual running of the show, falls into other hands: the mafia. Not even the America's Cup could avoid a scandal a few years ago when the race was held in the Sicilian port city of Trapani and lucrative deals were cut with government officials for the Cosa Nostra to gain huge windfalls of cash, both in construction contracts and, just for kicks, the nebulous realm of "entertainment."

You have two choices if you want to place major action on a yacht race. You can either shout across your bow at the captain of international industry anchored just adjacent to you, or you make a call to someone like Christopher Bonaventura. Bonaventura—or someone like him, since there are a hundred men just like him in Miami alone, never mind Italy—will give odds and take proposition wagers, and will treat you like the king you might very well be. If you're a billionaire, dealing with someone like Bonaventura isn't really like getting yourself involved in organized crime, since in your case, it's truly a victimless crime. You win, he pays. You lose, you pay. No one ends up getting their legs broken. It's a world of high-stakes betting by people who can afford to lose.

Which made figuring out who was pressuring Gennaro all the more difficult.

Kidnapping an heiress and her daughter in order to ensure a race's outcome is like setting fire to the Amazon to make s'mores: It would work, but it's a might excessive.

"I've never understood why anyone bothers with kidnappings anymore," Fiona said. "They so rarely work and then there's all that care and feeding that must take place so your captive doesn't die before you're ready to kill them. Or, worse, they have a heart attack or a stroke and you're left with some dreadful mess."

"You're a tender person, Fi," I said.

"Seriously, Michael, if you are the type of person to kidnap someone, you're ill equipped to care for your captive, which is only going to lead to bigger problems. It's so much easier to just do identity theft these days. You never have to worry about some sweating, crying child making a mess on your sofa or in the trunk of your car."

"You should film a public service announcement," I said.

"Would you want to spoon-feed some terrified person? Walk them to the bathroom? Beat them if you have to, which, as I think you can attest, is not as much fun as it seems? No, thank you," she said.

"Anyway," I said, "in this case, as of right now, Maria and Liz don't know any different. They're somewhere in the Atlantic, eating lobster off Wedgwood."

"That's a lot of trouble just to get some money."

"But that's the thing. If they wanted money, they could have yanked the diamonds out of Maria's ears. There's something else here."

Fi was still looking at the photo of Bonaventura. "Am I going to get to play with him?"

"I don't know yet," I said.

"That is a lovely suit."

"Fi."

"I'm just saying, Michael, that if given the chance and I need to execute him, we might remember to ask him for his tailor's name before he expires."

We pulled up in front of my mother's house. She was standing on the front porch, smoking and talking to a woman who looked vaguely familiar, in the way that many old women in Florida look vaguely familiar: She was wearing a white blouse that had a lovely multicolored pelican stitched over the right breast pocket, her hair was somewhere between blond and the color of an old French horn and was done in such a way that it looked strangely translucent. Even from the car, I could see that her lips had a lacquering of bloodred lipstick. She looked like a person wearing a Halloween costume of an Old Woman from Florida.

"Who is that?" I asked Fiona, since over the course of the last several months she'd gotten to know many of my mother's friends by virtue of attending Ma's weekly poker nights, the cooking course they took together and, frighteningly, for a time, a silent movie night at the Luart Theatre.

"That could be Esther," Fiona said. "But I don't think Esther would wear a pelican. She's always struck me as more of a seagull or egret type. So it might also be Doris. Or Cloris. They're sisters. Neither can bluff. But they play the river like pirates."

"Why does she look like that?"

"That's what all women look like after age 70, Michael, to punish men like you for disregarding women like me in our prime," she said and then got out of the car before I could respond, which was fine, because I didn't have a response.

I reached into the backseat and grabbed the Crock-Pot and the toaster oven, made a silent vow to myself to be pleasant and then got out of the car and walked up the front lawn toward the house.

When I reached them, Fiona was already in the middle of hugs and kisses from my mother and warm handshakes from the woman dressed like a drag queen. I set the boxes down and tried to look dutiful.

"Loretta," Ma said to the woman, all pretense of joy gone, "this is my son Michael. He's the one who works in shipping and receiving."

Passive.

Aggressive.

My mother.

"A pleasure," I said, and shook Loretta's hand, which was like shaking a leather bag filled with chicken bones.

Loretta looked me over with what could only be called disappointment. "My son works in Tallahassee," Loretta said.

"That's great to hear," I said.

"For the governor," she said.

"Even better."

"Michael, Loretta just moved in across the way. I've been telling her all about you."

"I see that," I said.

"Your mother says you help people," Loretta said.

I smiled. I envisioned helping Loretta's son out of a life of public service by virtue of the wholesale carpet bombing of Tallahassee, which, as far as capital cities goes, is about as aesthetically pleasing as a bleeding cyst. I smiled some more. I pushed my sunglasses up the bridge of my nose. And then I spoke, as calmly as possible.

"My mother overestimates my abilities," I said.

"I have a package that needs to get to Milton-Freewater overnight," Loretta said.

"Pardon me?"

"Your mother said you worked for—who was it, Madeline?"

My mother took a puff on her cigarette and really pondered the question. "Well, he doesn't like to talk about it. Do you, Michael?"

"No," I said. I looked at Fiona, tried to curry a little sympathy for the torture, but she was enjoying this far too much. There's not a lot of sympathy that exists in Fiona.

"Was it FedEx?" Loretta said. "Or those brown people?"

"That's them," my mother said. She jabbed her cigarette at me in affirmation. "UPS, right, Michael?"

My mother would have made an excellent counterterrorism operative. You want to stop a terrorist cell from pouring polonium into the water supply? Need to stifle an assassination plot? Have to secure a booby-trapped bridge? Just drop my mother into the center of activity and by day's end she'd have guilted every single person into passivity.

"That's right, Ma," I said. "If you have a package I can deliver, why, Loretta, you just leave it on the trunk of my car and I'll make sure it gets where it needs to go in twenty-four hours or less, or I'll refund your money."

"I'll do that," Loretta said. She looked over at the Charger, back at me, briefly at Fiona, and then paused with a finger to her upper lip, seemingly confounded by something just out of her mental reach, which, if pressed, I'd say was the majority of human knowledge. "Would you like me to see if there are any openings in the mailroom where my son works?"

"That's okay," I said. "I love my job."

"That car is a hazard. And the gas prices you're paying, well, you're leaving quite the carbon foot-print."

"I'm fine," I said.

"My son, he's an accountant. He could look at your finances."

"Is he single?" Fiona asked.

"Oh, no," she said. "He likes women with some meat on their bones, not you South Beach types." Loretta reached over and gave Fiona's waist a pinch, causing Fi to emit a high-pitched squeal. People have lost the ability to walk for less. "If you turn to the side, no one can see you. No offense."

"None taken," Fi said, but it was in a tone of voice that indicated to me that we were all about ten seconds away from being party to a homicide.

I gave my mother a look meant to alert her of that very thing, but she was already in motion.

"Loretta was just leaving," Ma said, and gave her new neighbor a slight push on the small of her back, like you would a puppy who wasn't getting outside fast enough.

"I thought we were going to play canasta," Loretta said.

"Can't you see my son is here? We'll play some other time."

We stood on the porch and watched Loretta walk across the street, which was a long and arduous process.

"She seems nice," I said.

"She's a pill," my mother said with absolutely no emotion at all. She reached down and picked up one of the boxes. "Is this the act of contrition or is it the other one?"

"I bought both of them prior to lunch," I said.

"Well, bring them in and I'll make some coffee while you apologize to me."

Two hours, a fixed halogen lamp first purchased when men in Miami were wearing pink T-shirts and white blazers, the systematic removal of spoiled food from the refrigerator (my mother had a veritable museum devoted to discontinued Swanson chicken TV dinners deep in the permafrost of her freezer) and two bags of leaves raked from the backyard later, and I had served my penance.

All while Fi and my mother sat on the sofa, reading magazines and watching Gary Coleman's *E! True Hollywood Story.*

"He hated his mother, too," my mother said, pointing at the television.

"I don't hate you, Ma," I said. Though I was now covered in sweat and smelled vaguely like a mixture of freezer burn and mulch, which didn't exactly turn on the warm part of my heart. It was a little too much like when Nate and I were kids and we'd wake up to find a to-do list on the kitchen counter that consisted of the sort of chores perhaps best done by a crew of adult men.

You've not lived until you've fallen from a palm tree with a saw in your hand.

Even then, I didn't actually break my leg.

"I feel . . . frustrated . . . occasionally by you, but that's not hate, Ma."

"I wanted to talk about that," she said.

This was about to be bad news.

"Ma," I said, "I've got a busy week ahead of me. Right, Fi?"

"I'm not privy to your intimate plans, Michael," Fiona said.

My mother ignored us both. "I've made us an appointment."

"I'm not going to any more therapy appointments," I said.

"This isn't therapy," she said. "Loretta said she and her son really connected after seeing this woman."

I looked at Fiona for support, but she wasn't giving any indication that she cared. She was back to being riveted by Gary Coleman. "What a strange little man," she said. You grow up in Ireland, the easiest things capture you.

"You said yourself that woman is a pill."

"But she and her son have a wonderful relationship."

"So do you and Nate," I said.

My mom frowned.

I know how to speak more languages than a translator at the UN. I can shoot someone between the eyes from half a mile away. If I'm shackled to an anchor and dropped overboard in the Caspian Sea, provided the currents are light and I've got a paper clip, I can be free and swimming the backstroke in thirty seconds.

But I don't know how to diffuse my mother's frown. Didn't at ten. Don't now.

"I thought we were done with this stuff," I said. "You kicked the last therapist out of the house."

"I think your recovery has hit a bump. They said it would happen."

"Who are 'they'?"

"Well, on television. There's a reality program about just this sort of thing and they say that people frequently return to their problems. They call it backsliding."

"There's a reality show about a spy whose mother makes him go to therapy?"

"Michael, the point is you have to deal with your addiction."

"I'm not addicted to anything, Ma. What is this show?"

"It follows drunks around and such. But the parallels are very clear to me and would be to you, too. Anyway, this isn't about healing; it's about bonding. We don't ever bond, Michael. We just fight over the past and I'm tired of it. We need to make new memories."

"How do you make a new memory? By definition, a memory has already happened."

"For someone so worldly, you're awfully naive about the way real people think," she said.

I exhaled, which was good because I'd been holding my breath without even knowing it. Sometimes, it's just easier not to breathe around my mother. It reminds me that things could be worse. I could be buried alive, for instance.

"When?" I said.

"End of the week."

"What time?"

"One. We'll get lunch first. There's a charming diner just across the street where Loretta says you can get soy smoothies."

"You don't even like soy," I said. I had doubts she knew what it was, but I decided to keep that to myself.

"Michael, I'm making the effort," she said.

"If I'm busy," I said, "I'll call you."

"What could you possibly be doing?"

Just as I was about to explain to my mother the entirety of the possibilities, I was saved by the ringing of my cell phone. It was Sam.

"Mikey," he said, "there's been a slight change of plans." His voice sounded a touch on the anxious side. If there's one thing to know about Sam Axe, he doesn't get overly anxious.

"We didn't have any plans, Sam."

"Right. That's the change."

"Where are you?"

"Incognito."

"A little more specific, Sam?"

"About a hundred meters from your mother's house, watching the person watching you."

I walked across the living room, out the front door and onto the porch. On the trunk of my car was Loretta's package, which was wrapped with so much tape that I could actually see my reflection in it. I looked down both sides of the street. Nothing. "I don't see you," I said.

"That's because I'm a highly trained operative, Mike," he said. "Do you see the Lexus parked on the other side of the stop sign to your southeast?"

I turned and casually gazed down the street behind me, gave a hearty belly laugh and patted the top of my head like a trained monkey, all while staring at a car in the wrong neighborhood. The last time someone pulled down this street in a silver Lexus IS and parked under a shady tree for the afternoon . . . well, they were probably looking for me, too. This is a Dodge and Honda street, and Honda had to muscle its way in.

Inside the car was a man trying to look inconspicuous, which is difficult when the burned spy you're watching is looking right at you and could, if he wanted, pull you from the car by your eyebrows.

"Who is he?" I asked, still in full laugh. Just having a nice day on the front lawn. Inhaling the humidity. Enjoying the clouds in the sky. Having a pleasant conversation with my buddy the ex–Navy SEAL about the meathead in a Lexus and relishing the start of hurricane season.

"I'm not sure," Sam said. "I've got a buddy running the plates now. But he isn't one of ours. Not a Fed boy."

"No," I said, "the Lexus gives that away. When did you pick him up?"

"I didn't," he said. "I came here to give you the news on what I'd found out about Gennaro's problem and saw him. You want me to bring the wrath of Neighborhood Watch Commander Chuck Finley upon him?"

I looked around again to see if I could locate Sam. He was really hiding quite well, though his tendency to wear floral prints was probably helping the situation here in the land of palm trees and birds of paradise.

"Give me a minute to get back inside," I said.

"Got it," Sam said.

Just as I started to walk back toward the house, Loretta came sprinting—well, comparatively speaking—from across the street, her pelican shirt buttoned haphazardly, her hair in a set of rollers, a single word bursting from her in a fracture of frenzied repetition: "PERVERT! PERVERT! PERVERT!"

"Sam?"

"CALL NINE-ONE-ONE. CALL NINE-ONE-ONE. CALL NINE-ONE-ONE . . ."

"I'm Oscar Mike," Sam said, slipping into the military parlance for, essentially, "on the move," which was fine since the Lexus was officially Oscar Mike, too.

"Great," I said. "Tell me she didn't see your face."

"Impossible," he said. He didn't sound terribly convincing, which might have been because he was sprinting away from his previous location, which I suspect was somewhere near Loretta's bathroom, judging by the way she was screaming, the status of her hair and her difficultly in putting her clothing back on correctly.

"Let me diffuse this before my mother calls in an airstrike," I said.

"PERVERT! IN MY BACKYARD! PERVERT! CALL NINE-ONE-ONE!"

"I'll meet you back at the loft," he said. "We've got a few, uh, problems I need to fill you in on."

"Of course you do," I said.

"Oh, and Mikey? Maybe stay away from any-one who looks like they might be, you know, *gang affiliated* between now and when we meet up."

"PERVERT! DO YOU HEAR ME? PERVERT!"

Loretta was only a few feet away from me and gaining as quickly as a snail might gain on a cheetah. "Tell me you didn't tweak Bonaventura," I said.

"Ah, Mikey, it was just one of those things that happens unexpectedly in the course of gathering information," Sam said.

"Like peeping on someone's grandmother, Sam?"

"I didn't see a thing," Sam said, "and I'll take that to the grave."

"ARE YOU CALLING NINE-ONE-ONE?"

"You might have to," I said.

"I'll fill you in," he said, "but right now I've gotta jump over a fence guarded by a pair of vicious-looking poodles." Working with Sam was like working with a meat grinder: The end result tended to be palatable, but getting there occasion-ally involved a bit more blood and guts than you might expect. "And hey, Mikey? I need you to re-mind me never to get dentures, okay?"

6

There's no such thing as an entirely safe Web site. There are levels of security, firewalls and booby traps and encrypted trapdoors that will send a rank amateur back to his single bed in his mother's basement, but for anyone with a dedicated desire to break into a site, nothing is impossible. You don't need to be a spy, or even of voting age, to figure out how to dismantle what one would presume to be the most secure sites.

NASA?

The Pentagon?

Both were hacked by the same fifteen-year-old boy, Jonathan James. A few years later, NASA, the Navy, the Energy Department and Jet Propulsion Laboratory were all hacked by the same twenty-year-old Romanian, Victor Faur. At the same time, NASA was being hacked by an unemployed British man named Gary McKinnon, who was looking for evidence of extraterrestrial life . . . and was doing it from his girlfriend's aunt's bedroom, which isn't exactly like working out of Quantico.

Hacking into the highest levels of American government doesn't require an MIT education, not if your girlfriend's aunt has a broadband connection, and not if you know even a little bit about moving around encryption devices and have a good understanding of how to rewrite programs to work for you, not against you.

Sam doesn't have an MIT education, either. He doesn't mainline Red Bull. He's not prone to wearing jaunty capes while discussing his favorite manga characters with his buddies in his parents' basement. He's done some "special projects" for the government, so he knows his way around a computer, but doesn't have the skills to hack his own bank to move a few zeros around, much less search for the existence of space aliens on NASA's Web site. So while I'd been busy cleaning my mother's house that morning, Sam was trying to work a few contacts who could take a look at the Web site streaming the video of Gennaro's wife and daughter. He probably didn't plan on eventually scaring a half-naked grandmother out of her house a few hours later, but then not all days go exactly how you plan them.

Which is how he ended up having a breakfast date at the Roasters 'n' Toasters deli on South Dixie Highway with a former NSA basement dweller named Walt. He'd called Walt the night previous in hopes of handling things on the phone, but Walt was one of those old-school guys who liked to be face-to-face, though Sam got the impression the guy just wanted a free meal. The more aggravating aspect was that Walt, now that he was retired, thought meeting somewhere at six a.m. was perfectly normal. Sam hoped that once his pension came in, he wouldn't be one of those people. He didn't want to see six a.m. unless he was creeping up behind it on the way home.

But there Sam sat, surrounded by a breakfast gang that seemed to know each other intimately. Sharing newspapers. Bitching about the Democrats. Drinking coffee like their prostates were made of Teflon. Not a Bloody Mary or Mimosa to be found, which Sam considered a punishable offense.

"You come here a lot?" Sam asked.

"Every morning," Walt said. "Most of the people here are ex-military or government. It's a good crowd."

"Just so I understand," Sam said, "you spent thirty years in the NSA so you could retire, move to Miami and surround yourself with all of the same people?"

"You want that I should have gone to San Francisco and moved into some liberal hippie commune?"

Sam liked Walt, thought he was a nice enough fellow, a good American, all that, but he got the feeling Walt hadn't turned on a television since Reagan left office. That wasn't punishable, but watching him eat runny scrambled eggs might have been, which he'd been doing for the last fifteen minutes. Three times the waitress had brought over a plate of eggs, and three times Walt had sent it back after a few bites, saying the consistency wasn't right, until finally the waitress brought over a serving that made Sam seriously ponder vegetarianism for a few moments.

"All that's missing are the feathers," Sam said.

"You overcook scrambled eggs," Walt said, "you lose all the iron."

Sam didn't think that was true, didn't even know if eggs contained iron, but at this point didn't even really care. Two Tums from now and this whole nauseating aspect of the experience would be rectified. Besides, there wasn't a better computer security guy in all of Miami than Walt, even though by the looks of him now, in his country club windbreaker and yellow polo shirt, he was probably spending most of his time on a putting green. He was one of those guys who looked like he was fifty when he was twenty-five, from all that time spent sitting around dark rooms, analyzing data on a computer screen, which made Sam wonder just how old Walt really was, since now the poor guy looked damn near dead, albeit relaxed, in his new retired state. He noticed Walt even had dentures now. Weird, because the last time they'd done work together was just a few months previous, and the guy had a full mouth of god-given teeth.

"Listen, Big Walt," Sam said, "I've got a top-secret mission I need some help on."

"If it's so top secret," Walt said, "why are you coming to a private citizen like me?"

"That's how secret it is," Sam said, "even people in government are suspect."

That seemed to satisfy Walt, or at least found a spot in his ego that was sufficiently inured from actual truth. Anyway, working with ex-NSA guys was always a bit of a pain in the ass. They just knew a lot more than other people. But that was okay, Sam thought, since it gave someone like Walt something to be proud of in addition to his penchant for eating, essentially, the moderately warmed ovum of a chicken. And it wasn't like Walt was feeding information directly to Rumsfeld back when they were both still employed, anyway. Walt's job was your basic low-level computer security gig at the NSA, like tracking minor threats on things like the Eastern Interconnected System power grid and calls about suspected terrorists with MySpace pages. Nine to five, no weekends, no direct knowledge of Dick Cheney's whereabouts at any given time, but a business card that said NSA, which was pretty good for getting people to waive late charges at Blockbuster.

Sam showed Walt the Web site and the video,

which Sam noted had been updated since the night before. There was even more footage now.

"Don't tell me this is some kind of pornography," Walt said, shoving Sam's laptop away at the first sight of the woman and child.

"No, no, nothing like that," Sam said.

"Because I'm here to tell you that pornography leads to terrorism. Studies have proven this."

The other pain-in-the-ass aspect of working with ex-NSA is that a lot of them were desperately odd people who'd spent their best years scared out of their minds by the shit they'd witnessed, even if they witnessed it on the computer or through secondary reports.

"Agreed, totally," Sam said. Sometimes it's just better to not argue over the peccadilloes of the retired. Sam explained to Walt the bare bones of the issues—which is to say he decided to just make everything up. "The woman in this video is the princess of Moldavia, as you know," he said, "and we have reason to believe that she's being tracked by Carpathians intent on harming her and her crown. But it's not entirely certain where these evildoers are currently operating out of."

Walt nodded and took another mouthful of egg and then broke off a piece of toast and dunked it into the liquid. "Interesting," he said. "Haven't seen anything on the news about this."

"Very hush-hush," Sam said. When he'd done some work with Walt in the past, he was upset to learn that Walt was one of those people who liked to lecture others about alcohol consumption before certain hours, which was too bad since Sam now couldn't get it out of his mind what an injustice it was that he was up this early and couldn't reasonably order a Bloody Mary without drawing undo attention. Sam thought it would make this meeting a lot less mentally taxing, never mind dulling the sounds of Walt's chewing, which included a troubling amount of whistling. "I need to get some tracking on this site, get an idea of who is viewing it, who is uploading it, access points, whatever you can find out. The safety of Moldavia depends on it."

Sam couldn't remember if Moldavia was a real country or if it had something to do with the Ice Princess from *General Hospital* back in the day, a brief addiction he'd unabashedly had while recovering from a bullet wound. Anyway, it didn't seem like Walt knew, either, since he took Sam's laptop and started typing absently on the keyboard with one hand, the other still busy with breakfast. After about ten minutes of this one-handed show, which also involved Walt making a weird clicking noise with his tongue against the roof of his dentures, he set the laptop aside.

"A decent IT guy will see someone breaking into this site in fifteen seconds."

Sam was afraid of that. Technology has a way of passing you by if you're busy getting dentures and playing golf. He really had to ask him about the denture thing. It was quite curious, since the NSA had a helluva health plan. "I understand," Sam said. "You know someone else I could talk to?"

"No need," Walt said. He pushed the laptop across the table. "I already got you the information."

Cagey bastard.

Sam clicked through the files. It was a pretty extensive array, considering Walt managed to literally get it all with one hand.

"Impressive," Sam said. There were almost fifteen pages of information stored now, but Sam couldn't figure out what he was looking at, as most of it consisted of lines of letters and numbers that reminded him of launch codes.

"You don't just lose it," Walt said.

"What do we have here?"

"Everything. Lots of stuff for you to chew on."

Sam considered that for a moment in light of all the information he'd gleaned just by looking at Walt. "What happened with your teeth?"

"Got tired of 'em," he said. "One less thing to worry about. That's the great thing about being retired. You get to make your own decisions about what you want to spend your time obsessing about. Mark my words. Day you retire, you'll start thinking about getting rid of your chompers, too."

Sam found that hard to believe. If he was going to get some kind of body modification, he might go for a robotic arm that fired missiles, or see about what a hollow leg would actually cost, or just go straight toward the Superman route and get X-ray vision, which would be pretty useful living in Miami. But his teeth were staying put. In the spirit of being fraternal, however, Sam thought he'd ask Walt for the name of his dentist at some point so Walt wouldn't feel like Sam was just using him for his technological expertise.

"Tell me something, Walt," Sam said. "This system you just cracked. How much would someone spend to set something like this up?"

Walt ran his tongue over the front of his "teeth" and thought about it for a moment. "Whoever did the work on this was pretty sharp," he said. "And getting through the Italian was a challenge. Don't Moldavians speak Moldavees?"

"Usually." Sam was beginning to sense that Walt was slightly more versed in world history than previously assumed. "But they are a crafty people. Heavy on the linguistics."

"Whoever set this up had decent training," Walt said. "Even had a good idea of how an attack might come. Very interesting in terms of the flanking they did, but it's about six months out of date. Lots of holes, if you know what to look for. But then, I'm former NSA." Walt's voice rose when he said *former NSA*, which Sam thought was probably a good way to get comped desserts and such. He made a mental note to play up his SEAL experi-

-ence next time he was a little short on cash at a restaurant, see if he couldn't get some sugar for his troubles.

"My guess?" Walt continued. "Whoever did this had some serious coin behind them. I cross-site scripted the mother without much problem, but I've got full faith and credit behind me."

If you're not interested in a long-term campaign of technoterrorism, or aren't interested in finally learning if the truth is out there concerning the aliens, JFK and the existence of Bigfoot, and merely want to track the movements of those behind the screen and anyone who might be visiting the Web site you've staked out, the best way is via cross-site scripting.

If you're trying to break into the CIA, it's unlikely cross-site scripting will help you, because they already have it on their site to track you, but if you're attempting to sneak inside open-source platforms like blogging shells or social networking sites, or a Web site set up by kidnappers to show a single video, you have a better chance of getting in and out without detection at least once.

All you have to do is inject a line of malicious code into a part of the Web site that you know is being viewed. Once the object is viewed—in this case, the video—the code leaches information from the viewer. A porn site might just want to know your e-mail address so it can bombard you with messages for penis-enlargement surgery, but a gambling site might start rooting through your computer for banking information; an identity thief might want to inhabit your life entirely.

Since the Web site with the video was a closed circle, it was easy for Walt to put the code inside the video player once he was able to slide past the security checkpoints, which Sam figured he did about midway through a mouthful of hash browns, and find out who else was viewing the site apart from Gennaro. . . . Or at least where they were viewing it from.

"Can you give me an idea what I'm looking at here?" Sam asked.

Walt exhaled hard through his mouth, which sounded like the opening strains of "Yankee Doodle Dandy" as it whistled through his gum line. "You've got three users on this Web site," he said. "Four counting us." He sounded frustrated, like Sam should have been able to figure that out on his own, which maybe he could have if he'd not bothered to have a life all these years. That was one other thing about working with these ex-NSA computer guys, Sam realized; they used their geek factor against you. "Two of them are in Miami using the same wireless IP. One of them, the person actually maintaining the site, is smart enough to use a proxy server, but not smart enough to use a good proxy server." He typed a few things into the laptop again and then smiled. "Corsica. The other person is in Corsica."

Mounting an armored assault on the island of Corsica didn't seem like a real possibility, so Sam chose to focus on the two people in Miami.

"Can you pinpoint where, exactly, the people in Miami are?"

Walt sighed, like he couldn't believe Sam would ask him such a stupid question. He had a lot of ego for a guy with no teeth, but a few seconds of clicking delivered Sam the answer he was afraid of. "This is the IP for the Setai Hotel."

A part of Sam sort of wished it was Madonna who was putting the screws to Gennaro, but he had a pretty good idea that the Material Girl wasn't in the kidnapping business. But then he couldn't imagine anyone else with the cash to stay at that hotel who would be, either.

"One other thing," Sam said. "In light of the recent information here, and as it relates to the safety of Moldavia, could you sweep into the Setai's reservation system and get me a list of names of the people staying there?"

"That's illegal," Walt said.

"No, no," Sam said. "This has all been cleared by the top levels of Her Majesty's Royal Guard. We have nothing to worry about. So quick like a bunny, before the princess dies, get me that list, will you?"

A few seconds later, and after much heavy breathing from Walt, as if he were really exerting himself and not just typing, Sam had a list of more than a hundred names open on his computer, along with all of their salient information. He recognized a few names—Madonna was staying on the eleventh floor and had ordered a lovely lobster ravioli for lunch; Al Pacino was on the fifteenth but was checking out this afternoon, which was good since he was already three hundred dollars in the red on valet fees; and Carson Daly was staying on the twenty-first, which seemed silly compared to the relative fame of the others, but Sam figured maybe Daly required less oxygen to survive—but no other names jumped out directly. He'd get a buddy at the FBI to run the list, anyway, see if anyone showed up as wanted for anything interesting.

He wasn't even sure who he hoped to find on the list, since it's not as if there were bands of famous kidnappers floating around. Sam couldn't even think of anyone who did it regularly and with much success apart from, well, Hezbollah, but he didn't think they were in the market for Italian heirs.

He scanned back over the list one more time and landed on one curious name: Nicholas Dinino, Gennaro's father-in-law. Nicholas was staying in the other penthouse suite just adjacent to Gennaro's, which made sense. It didn't mean anything insidious. They were family, after all, but in the scope of the information Walt had just delivered, it felt . . . curious.

"*Quid pro quo*," Walt said, and Sam immediately cursed the existence of that Hannibal Lecter movie that taught everyone the term *quid pro quo*. More than fifteen years later, and half the universe was still tossing it around like it meant something. Combine that with "Man up!" and "Wassup?" and "You go, girl!" and Sam was pretty sure that most of the people he came into contact with only said things parroted from morons and beer commercials. Not that there was anything wrong with beer commercials conceptually, just that they weren't especially deep with philosophical thought and nuance.

"Sure, Walt."

Walt smiled, which made Sam recoil. Man, those teeth looked strange. They were just too white, and his gums were too pink and his tongue, well, his tongue was too gray. Sam made a mental note that when he retired he was going to brush his teeth three times a day, just to make up for whatever karmic tarnishing was going on this day. "You think you could take out my neighbor's parakeet? It chirps all night long and keeps me up like you wouldn't believe."

"I'm not in the assassination business," Sam said, and Walt seemed disappointed.

"Well, next time," he said.

Next time, Sam thought, he'd ring up a different buddy.

Sam's original plan was to make some phone calls about the list of names, but it was too damn early. It wasn't even seven thirty a.m. by the time he got out of Roasters 'n' Toasters, which just wasn't right. Who retires so they can wake up at the ass-crack of dawn? He'd go to the Carlito, but he still had another three and half hours before the doors opened and the scenery picked up.

Besides, he had a niggling sense that something just wasn't adding up about the names on the list, even before calling on them. If Christopher Bonaventura were in town, wouldn't he be staying at a place like the Setai? Sam didn't think a guy like Bonaventura would have the moxie to set up a Web site as first-rate as the one he'd just viewed, nor did he really think Bonaventura was behind the kidnapping in the first place, but he figured that getting a jump on the other side of the problem with Gennaro would solve some issues later on, so he called the one buddy he knew who might be up at this early hour and who might know where to find visiting mafia dignitaries.

Darleen worked organized crime in New York when Sam first met her, and he was pretty sure they had a night of passion right around the turn of the millennium, back when everyone—

especially everyone who was privy to inside information about what they feared was likely to be the total destruction of the American infrastructure—thought they could write checks that would never be cashed. Fact was, he just wasn't 100 percent certain about it. It was a long night. There were several bottles of champagne involved, and all of it happened in an unmarked building in Newark that housed an alphabet soup of secret agencies. Nothing good ever happened in Newark, though technically, neither of them were even there. Anyway, she'd never mentioned it and he'd never mentioned it, and that was okay. Sam didn't think that if his performance had been notable there would be this silence, so he thought not poking a stick into the issue was likely to keep the specter of disappointment away from both of them.

At any rate, Darleen was now working in Miami, proctoring the old-school five families, the new-school Russians and Cubans, the executive branches of the Bloods, Crips and Mexican Mafia, and whoever else came along through the Port of Miami wanting to organize and do crime. It meant she had a lot of late nights that looked like early mornings, so he wasn't too worried about calling her before eight. Though as he dialed her number, he tried to figure out what she looked like at eight a.m. from his previous recollection, but just kept coming up with the sensation of pain in the back of his skull, which was likely a champagne hangover flashback and not anything exciting or acrobatic being conjured.

"Sam Axe," Darleen said, "I must say I wasn't expecting a call from you this fine morning. You locked in a cell in Kabul or something?"

"No, no," Sam said, "I'm just picking up a protein shake and then heading off for my morning ocean swim."

"I'd like to see that," Darleen said.

Sam wanted to believe she was being flirtatious, but he got the sense that she was being facetious. Maybe he was wrong about that night. That whole "partying like it was 1999" business did tend to dull the old cerebrum. "Listen, Darleen, small favor."

"Small?"

Hmmm. Now he really wasn't sure. There was a lot of subtext to this woman. A lot of levels. A lot of ramps. He started thinking of her like a parking garage and realized it was really far more than he could reasonably be asked to deal with before noon. Tough to be really smooth when Regis and Kelly are still on in most houses. Never mind he'd already spent far too long talking to Walt, which was like intellectual antifreeze.

"Yeah," he said. "Tiny." Be humble, he thought, just go with it. "I'm trying to track down Christopher Bonaventura. You got any idea where I might be able to find him this week?"

There was a pause on the other end of the line, a change in the energy of the phone call, and Sam recognized that dropping Bonaventura's name into the middle of a nice chat that may or may not have been reflective of a brief sexual liaison about a decade ago might have been a surprise. "You've got no reason to be looking for Christopher Bonaventura."

Normally, Sam liked that kind of direct talk. Simple orders. *Do this. Do that. Put it there.* Nice thing about being a SEAL was that you pretty much always knew how your boss felt about you and what was expected of you; there was not a lot of emotional negotiation. But this was more like a personnel directive from human resources, both for today and tomorrow and probably the foreseeable future.

"I don't even need to talk to him," Sam said. "I just need to know where he's staying while he's in town."

"Why would you think he's in town?"

The problem about digging a hole is that if you're not careful, someone is liable to push you into it.

"I saw that explosion yesterday and figured it had to do with him," Sam said. It was worth a shot, he figured, since Gennaro had mentioned it the night previous. And if Gennaro knew, well, then the FBI knew. And if the FBI knew, then everyone with a security clearance above a janitor at the field office over on Northwest 2nd Avenue probably already had a peek at the incident report. It was a nice office, really, with strong, sound-proof walls and a good location. There was a bar across the street called the Dorsal Fin where, for the price of a shot, and on a particularly slow news day, you could probably get a few mundane state secrets.

Darleen stayed silent. When she finally did speak, all she said was, "And?"

"And, well, I'm sort of working with a friend who has business interests affected by this terrible calamity," Sam said. When Darleen didn't reply immediately, he added, and kept adding and adding and adding, "And as you know, I'm concerned about the intercoastal byways and that was a significant environmental accident out there, which, when you take into consideration the migration patterns of the seagull, and the swallows of Capistrano which, as you know, are endangered, could be considered a problem. Internationally. As you know."

Sam was of the opinion that if you added the words "as you know" to anything, people tended to pretend as if they did know, if only to not seem comparatively ill informed. It was a skill he'd gleaned working with intelligence people. No one wants to seem like a moron, even if admitting they don't know something would likely make them seem all the more reliable.

"Sam," she said, "he got away with killing his own father. You don't just walk up and talk to him unless you have a good reason to have the mafia on your ass. These guys are true blood killers, not a bunch of Newark posers."

Newark.

Sam was pretty sure that was a signal.

Really, it didn't matter. He'd recently had a brush with unwanted marriage, and then there was the fact that he was technically still married to an ex-hippie, but it was useless to dwell on the past. Well, maybe not *useless*, but not advisable, anyway. Faced with dealing with history or dealing with the moment, Sam always advocated the moment. It was controllable. Besides, what was nice about his current position in life was that he got to spend a long time at the old romantic buffet, but even still you never knew when your favorite place might get shut down with an E. coli breakout. Or, in the case of Veronica, whom he didn't hate, certainly, just didn't want to, uh, spend forever with, another marriage proposal. Though he sure missed his Cadillac.

It was tough being a desirable man, Sam knew, but he wasn't Burger King—some people just weren't going to get it their way.

"All I'm asking is if you know where he's staying," Sam said. "I'm not planning on some Elliot Ness takedown."

Darleen kind of snorted in response. It was a

weird sound coming from a woman, but then he'd heard and seen a man whistle through his false teeth today without any sense of embarrassment in the least, which made Sam think that vanity was really an underrated thing. It wasn't even eight thirty in the morning and he was already having moments of clarity, and without any liquid encouragement.

Maybe he actually would start waking up and taking ocean swims.

Sam thought he'd try one more parry before giving up the whole story just to get an address. Worst case scenario, he'd just tell Darleen the truth. She was FBI, after all. If she really wanted the truth, she could probably get it without Sam ever knowing. "Look, fact is, it's not really for me. It's for a sick friend. He thinks Bonaventura might be the only person who has a matching bone marrow profile. Not even a natural-born killer can turn down someone in need of a little bone marrow. If I can make the effort to find him, well, I think Mr. Bonaventura might make the effort to help my friend."

That should do it, Sam thought. Find some middle ground. Appeal to her emotional center. Remind her of just how cuddly old Sam Axe was. Though the more he thought about it, he was starting to think that maybe the woman there that night in Newark was actually named Carlene.

"He has a compound that he uses on Key Biscayne," she said, though her voice sounded kind of robotic, like she was giving a report, but then gave Sam the address. "I wouldn't stop by with a scalpel and try to get that marrow out of him; you're likely to end up gator bait."

"Noted," Sam said.

"And Sam? Whoever is employing you? Tell his to pay his debt and get out of the country and then see about getting into the space program. Bonaventura is not the kind of person who chalks things up to being part of the game. It's all personal to him."

"Noted," Sam said. He wasn't sure why he kept saying *noted*, but he sort of thought it made him sound more official. "Anything else, Darleen?"

Sam could hear a light tapping sound, as if maybe Darleen was clicking her teeth together, getting pensive, thoughtful, conjuring that night in Newark herself. Sam Time *is* hard to forget. He imagined her sitting in her office and really trying to get a fix on her memories, maybe even pondering a meet up at the Dorsal Fin for a few drinks and then, well, why plan it?

He heard that tapping sound again and realized that was actually the sound of her typing in the background. "Yes," she said, "come to think of it, one other thing. *As you know*, having your friend Mr. Westen involved with Bonaventura would be bad for his profile. So I'd say it would be smart to be discreet."

Sam was always surprised by how much other people knew about his business. "Discreet it is," he said, and then made a mental note not to let Fiona set fire to anything valuable.

Most criminals like to keep a low profile. If you're a bank robber, the odds are you don't carry around a card that says BANKS KNOCKED OVER 24-7! If you're a serial killer, you probably don't run an ad on the back page of the *Miami New Times* offering severed heads for sale. Even if you're a hit man— a job predicated on people knowing about your services—it's fair to assume you're not standing on A1-A with a sandwich board offering your wares.

All of which made the house Christopher Bonaventura was staying in that much more sus- pect. It wasn't just the phalanx of black-on-black Mercedes-Benzes and Suburbans, with bulletproof body armor, encircling the drive that made it so suspect, though that certainly wasn't helping mat- ters; it was also the men standing behind the front gate of the house on Harbor Drive holding modi- fied M1911A1 .45s like they were rolling with a Marine Force Recon unit.

Thing of it was, Sam thought, they sort of looked like Marines, too. Close-cropped hair. Square jaws. Arms as thick as thighs. Used to be mafia foot soldiers were on the chunky side. It wasn't like they were big on hand-to-hand com- bat. They shot you or hit you in the head with a rock or clubbed you to death with a bat and then buried you in a cornfield. Physical work, sure, but quick work. Nothing where you'd need big muscle endurance. But these guys looked like they were hitting the free weights pretty regularly. Maybe taking a syringe or two, also, since Sam thought he could make out the entire arterial path of the guy closest to the gate and he wasn't even out of the car yet.

Despite Darleen's admonition to avoid it, Sam figured he'd drive by the house where Bonaventura was staying for the week, anyway, just to get the lay of the land, see what was what, and any other cliché he could think of. The truth was that he just wanted to see the damn place, since a house on Harbor Drive in Key Biscayne meant bucks he frankly didn't think even the mob could afford.

At least not publicly.

So now he was parked across the street from a house three stories tall with a visible tennis court on the roof, the mere idea of which made Sam wonder just how dedicated you have to be to a sport to put it on the roof of your house. Apart from the Benzes and Suburbans, it was about all he could really see from the street, since the front gate was thick black steel and the line of men behind it didn't exactly allow for great sight lines, at least not from across the street. So Sam got out of his car and started walking toward the house.

What was the worst that could happen? Sam thought it was unlikely that they'd open fire on him right away, plus it would be hard to explain the blood spatter all over the nice McMansion across the way. Gunfire on the nicest street in Key Biscayne was likely to cause a stir, so while these guys were strapped like they were expecting the Chinese Red Army to come stomping down the street, it was probably more about intimidation than action.

"Pardon me, boys," Sam said, "but I've lost my dog. Little cocker spaniel? White and sort of off-red. Party colored, they call 'em, but I just call him Chuck. You guys see anything matching that description?" The guys looked back and forth at each other with confusion, as if Sam were speaking gibberish, so he just kept walking toward the gate and talking. "Pink tongue, tends to poke out the side of his mouth when he's running? Just a nub of a tail? This sound familiar? Barks at every leaf and bug he sees? Anybody?" He kept phrasing everything like a question, thinking that eventually one of the guys holding the .45s would think to respond, if only to stop the cavalcade of queries.

He stopped talking when he got close enough to the gate that he could peer in rather easily, since now all of the guys were grouped together and muttering to each other in low voices Sam couldn't quite make out. He wasn't even really sure what he was looking for, but had a general feeling that because of the way things normally went down, he'd probably need to scale the wall and cause a ruckus at some point, so he might as well start looking for ways in now, before he was dodging bullets.

There was a sign in the middle of the gate that warned people away with threats of armed response units and fatal levels of electricity. If a dog really did get loose in this neighborhood and decided to raise his leg on Bonaventura's gate, he'd be electrocuted, which made Sam think that the wisdom behind HOAs was truly lost on the rich. Nevertheless, the guards didn't seem too concerned about the electricity, if their relative proximity to that gate was any judge.

Most people tend to shy away from electrified fencing, but the ten men assembled behind this one didn't seem to be too tense, which meant it was likely turned off. Maybe ten guys with guns and lethal electricity was considered overkill even for mob guys.

Sam counted up the cars. Five Suburbans, five Benzes, a few other dark black cars that didn't look quite so fortified, as well as three MV Agusta F4 CC motorcycles, a bike that runs around $130,000 out the door, and goes out that door at nearly two hundred mph. The aggregate value of the parked transportation was fairly mind-boggling. Really, being the good guys just didn't pay as well.

"No dog here," one of the guys said, but it was impossible to tell which one, since they all looked exactly the same: same hair, same facial features, same guns, probably the same flash grenades strapped to their chests, too. Whoever spoke did so in perfect, unaccented English. He might have been Italian, but he wasn't from Italy and didn't exactly fit the profile of someone who'd been cracking heads since getting "made."

"You sure? He's a gassy fella, so even if you didn't see him, you might smell him. Know what I mean?" Sam said. He was looking at one guy, the one he figured spoke to him a moment previous, but the answer came from a different person.

"You heard me," he said. "Now go. You're in the wrong neighborhood."

Testy.

"No, no, I live just down the block," Sam said. "Mind if I leave you my phone number? In case you see the dog, you could call me? My daughter and I, we, well, don't know what to do with ourselves. That dog has really helped my daughter with her, uh, spina bifida."

Sam wasn't sure what spinal bifida was, but figured it sounded just bad enough that not even these guys could turn away from it; testy demeanor or otherwise.

"Fine," the man said. "Give me your number." He pulled out a Talla-Tech RPDA-57, the official PDA of the Marines, a rugged green device that did everything from make calls to calibrate mortar coordinates. Not exactly the kind of thing you purchase at Office Depot. And not exactly the kind of thing mafia foot soldiers kept in their back pockets. If these men were employed by Christopher Bonaventura, it meant the game was a whole hell of a lot more complicated.

Sam gave the man his cell number and when the man asked him for his name, Sam said, "Chuck Finley."

For some reason, this got the men to exchange awkward glances with each other. Finally, Sam thought, old Chuck's getting a rep with the criminal element. . . .

"You said your dog's name was Chuck," the lone speaking man said.

Crap. Testy *and* paid attention. A Marine for sure.

"It is his name," Sam said. "It is. I love that mongrel so much I gave him my own name. It's easier for my daughter to remember, too. As you know, with spina bifida, the memory is often the first casualty, and with her mother gone, well, that dog is almost like another father to her."

All the men nodded in unison and with matching solemnity. It was like watching the Rockettes doing that kicking thing, and just as creepy. These guys might not be active service Marines, Sam thought, but they sure were regimented. And judging by their guns, PDAs and fresh haircuts, well funded. He just didn't have any idea what they were doing guarding Christopher Bonaventura's vacation house.

Or at least he didn't until Nicholas Dinino, Gennaro's stepfather-in-law, pulled up behind the men in a convertible Bentley Continental, waved innocuously as they opened the twin sides of the gate and then nearly ran Sam down as he sped away from the house.

7

When a spy decides to turn coat and start giving information to the enemy, it's rarely for the reasons you might expect. Most spies, if they choose to cross the aisle, do so of their own accord and not because they're being blackmailed. Cold War movies and spy thrillers always suggested that American agents were pushed into corners by grainy photos of illicit affairs, but the fact is that it's hard to trap a good spy in a blackmail scheme. If spies are worth turning, if they are at the level where they can provide truly useful information, pictures of them having sex with anyone or anything at any time and in any place will have no bearing on the situation.

Most spies that flip do it for one core reason: Money. Aldrich Ames ended up on the Russian payroll after he decided to divorce his wife and marry a Colombian woman with decidedly more expensive taste. So in order to pay off his debts, cover his alimony and lavish his new bride, he needed a quick capital infusion. First it was fifty thousand dollars for the names of several Soviets spying for the U.S.; then it was nearly $1.7 million for even more information once he realized that if you're going to go all in, you might as well go all in.

And if it's not money, it's ego ... with some money thrown in to sweeten the deal. Robert Hanssen needed money to pay for his children's expensive education, but most of all he wanted to feel valued for the work he'd done and wanted to get back at those who hadn't let him rise to the top echelons of the FBI. He wanted to feel valued. And what better way to feel valued then to have someone else tell you you're important, even if that someone is your blood enemy? An open checkbook is usually capable of changing long-held beliefs, even existential ones about love of country and patriotism and such, but it's hard to buy emotional relevance. That comes from a far stranger and more difficult place to locate.

When you cross your family, it's usually for similar reasons. Money, ego and twisted emotion make people do stupid things.

If you're essentially decent, maybe you end up hurting your mother's feelings on Mother's Day.

If you're essentially awful, maybe you orchestrate a kidnapping plot. If you're essentially awful and stupid, and not merely an opportunist, you orchestrate the plot in broad daylight and without concern for getting caught. It helps if you don't actually love the people you're screwing.

After hearing about Sam's morning of activity—and after spending time with my own mother—I was of the opinion that Gennaro Stefania was being manipulated for reasons far beyond simple yacht races and that he wasn't going to be able to make it all right by cleaning out the freezer.

Still, the perception of impropriety didn't make it true. It was perfectly reasonable to assume that Nicholas Dinino was going to Christopher Bonaventura's for reasons other than the planning and execution of nefarious deeds. They were both exceptionally rich men with common interests, which I explained to Sam and Fi as we stood in my kitchen a few hours after assuring Loretta, my mother and the entirety of their neighborhood that they didn't need to contact the governor's office to see if FEMA might pay for the emotional stress of Sam's prowling.

At some point, I had to see about getting my mother moved into a gated community somewhere in the Yucatán.

"Just because you saw Dinino going into Bonaventura's doesn't mean he's involved," I said. "We are dealing with some eccentric people here, Sam, who work in a lot of the same circles."

"He has a point," Fi said to Sam. "Look at the three of us. You might assume if you saw all of us together that we were planning some elaborate plot that would involve any number of crimes and misdemeanors, that would probably end up violating several people's civil rights, might even involve what I think they call domestic terrorism—right, Michael?"

"The difference is we're the good guys," I said. Fi raised her eyebrows. "Sam and I are, at any rate."

"You can put a killer whale in a tank at a zoo," Fi said, "can even train it to do adorable tricks and squirt water at people, but it's still a killer whale that would eat your face."

"I have a buddy who told me a story about that sort of thing," Sam said. He was relaxed and sipping on a beer but still had a few stray bits of leaf and grass stuck in his hair from his adventure in suburban surveillance. He had another unopened beer waiting on the counter, I guess to keep the other one company. "He said that if you keep those babies in captivity long enough, they'll just start feasting on human flesh."

"I am concerned that you have a buddy who knows that," I said.

"It's a vast network, Mikey. I have friends who don't even know they're my friends yet."

"Why do you think you have so many friends, Sam, and Michael has so few?" Fi said.

Sam shrugged. "I have a kinetic personality. People gravitate to me. You might say people like me."

"And I'm an acquired taste?" I said. Fi and Sam shared a look. It used to be that they never stood on the same side of any argument. Now they were practically Siamese twins. I decided to change the subject, permanently if possible. "Who was the guy outside my mother's house?"

"Weird thing," Sam said. He reached into his pants pocket and pulled out a scrap of paper that looked vaguely like the tag you might find on the back of a pillow. "The car is a rental, paid for with a corporate Visa by the Star Class Association."

"What's that? Some new CIA shell?" I said.

"I thought the same thing," Sam said. "But it checks out." He flipped the paper over and examined it closely. "It's one of the official sanctioning bodies for these yacht races Gennaro is in."

"What were they doing watching me?"

"I don't know," Sam said. "Maybe they have a security detail that was on you?"

"If they had a security detail," I said, "I would have spotted it. And they wouldn't have peeled out like that at the first sign of trouble." I thought about it for a moment. "You get a name on the rental?"

Sam flipped the paper over again. I could now make out the existing text. In bold letters across the top it said, DO NOT REMOVE. "The license they had on file is for Timothy Sherman."

"Any flags?"

"Only that it looks like he declined the extra insurance coverage he was offered and that he's letting people not on the rental agreement drive the car, since he's the license on ten different cars the group rented for the week. That's a pretty serious offense in the car rental business."

"Worse than ripping a warning tag from a mattress?" I said, pointing at the paper in Sam's hand.

"Technically," Sam said, "I got this off a duvet cover hanging on a line in Loretta's backyard, but I believe that's a state law. Lying on your rental agreement violates your own car insurance, so it's probably worse in the long run."

"We should execute him," Fiona said.

"We don't even know who he is," I said.

"Next of kin will show up to claim the body, and all of your questions will be answered." She picked up Sam's unopened beer and examined it closely, as if she wanted to make sure it didn't have cooties on it, and then opened it up and took a sip.

"That wasn't a twist top," Sam said.

"I have exceptionally strong wrists," she said.

"Instead of killing Mr. Sherman, maybe you could pay him a visit for me, Fi? Let him know he's violated his rental agreement? Tell him we need the proper names of who is operating the cars?"

Fi took another sip of beer and swallowed it with exaggerated brio. "Love to," she said. "But I have plans."

"Really?" I said.

"My friend who is visiting."

"The plutonium salesman?"

"He's not a salesman," she said. "More like a broker. And anyway, he said he didn't end up bringing it with him into the country. He said he'd rather just relax with a good friend and not be concerned about such trivial things."

"Like world security?"

"Like commerce," she said.

"Fi," I said. "I need your help here, and let's be honest, you haven't heard from the guy, have you?"

"Even if I haven't," she said, "there is the potential that I might." Fi took a long pull from her beer and then set it down. "Fine, but I demand handsome payment for this job."

"That's the other thing," Sam said. He went into what might graciously be called my bedroom, but which is just a mattress on the floor about three feet from my kitchen, and retrieved his laptop. Earlier, when I got back to the loft with Fi, Sam was napping beside the laptop and snoring like he had a trademark on sleep apnea. He explained to me then that he just wasn't physically constituted for early morning work and that I needed more lumbar support in my mattress.

"Let me guess," I said. "Gennaro is broke."

"Good guess," Sam said. "But not entirely accurate." Sam explained that he'd had his buddy

Jimenez—the guy who got us involved in this in the first place—get some information about the Ottone family fortunes after he saw Dinino roll up and learned that while Gennaro certainly had money, much of it was tied to his wife. They had a prenuptial that paid him handsomely in the event of their divorce—a million dollars for every year of marriage—but Gennaro's personal wealth was marginal in comparison and mostly generated from racing.

"Alone, he's worth maybe two million dollars," Sam said. "He owns the house he grew up in as a kid in California. That's worth seven hundred fifty K. He's got a few cars in his own name. A cabin in Tuscany. Keeps a small personal checking account. Everything else comes from the family. But he's on the books as the half owner of his team, but it's a paper ownership. He puts none of his own money in it, and when his team wins, which wasn't very often before this year, he cuts his share of the purse to his teammates. The largest part of the purse goes to the team owner, which, of course, is all in the family pot."

"Nice pot," Fi said.

"Where's the vast conspiracy, Sam?" I said.

"I was just getting to that," Sam said. He turned his laptop around. "That's Maria Ottone's will."

Fi scrolled through the pages. "It's a hundred pages long," she said. "I didn't know you could read that many pages at one time, Sam."

"I skimmed to the good parts," he said, and then told us what those were. If Maria died, her daughter stood as the chief beneficiary of her estate and Gennaro would be subject to the terms of the prenuptial, plus costs to take care of their daughter through age eighteen, when her full inheritance would be available. And if the daughter were to die, too? The money stayed in the family.

"And what if Gennaro dies?" I said.

"Mr. Dinino ends up with full ownership of the team and is married to a woman without an heir or anyone who might reasonably make a claim to her fortune."

"So," I said, "everyone dies and Dinino stands to make money he doesn't really need. Doesn't add up."

"That's why you're the spy," Sam said.

"There must be a girl involved," Fi said.

"Why?" I said.

"Because if there wasn't," she said, "no one would be acting this stupid."

It is always slightly frightening when Fiona is the voice of reason.

"What do we know about Dinino?" I said.

"Not a lot outside the public image," Sam said. "Married Maria's mother five years ago. Dated supermodels prior to that. Family was in the cement business before selling out a few years before Dinino married Mrs. Ottone. One ex-wife, still living. No children. No scandals apart from a class-action lawsuit over poor cement composition in 1988."

"No criminal involvement?"

"Nothing confirmed," Sam said. "But being in the cement business in Italy is a little bit like being in the trash business in Las Vegas. Even if you're not dirty, there's a good chance you're paying off someone to keep yourself clean."

"Might make sense for him to have some contacts like Bonaventura, then," I said. "Any reason to think he might be having money problems?"

"Apart from the wholesale crash of the world's financial markets last year?"

"Apart from that, yes."

"Seems solid."

"Trust me," Fi said. "At the end of this all, there will be a crying woman to blame."

"When was the last time you cried?" Sam asked.

Fiona thought for a moment. "It had to do with a pony. Do the math yourself."

"What did you get from the names of the people staying at the hotel?" I asked. "Anyone who might reasonably be going after Gennaro or the Ottones?"

Sam clicked open a new file on his computer. "Well, first thing, there's an insane amount of shrimp consumed by the guests of the Setai."

"If the crustaceans attack, we'll know why," I said. "What else?"

"No obvious red flags," he said, "except for the movies Carson Daly rented."

Sam went down the list of names and noted that in addition to half a dozen celebrities in for the week, there were also a good thirty private security personnel staying, too, including the bodyguards that normally travel with Nicholas Dinino.

"Why didn't we see any of them last night?" I said.

"Maybe they were hiding," Fi said. She dusted off Sam's second beer and was now poking around my cabinets for food. Something about this sort of talk always seemed to make Fiona hungry, which was funny since violence tended to make her aroused in an entirely different way. Figuring out Fiona's wiring would require a forensic neuropsychologist who also knew how to fight.

"I would have seen them," I said.

"You didn't see the man this morning," she said. She found a box of saltines and was now back in the fridge. "Do you keep any kind of spreads, Michael? Butter? Jam? Nutella?"

"No."

"What do you put on these crackers?"

"Nothing," I said. "They were here when I moved in." Fiona tossed the box in the trash and opted for my last serving of blueberry yogurt. "And I would have seen the man on my mother's street if I hadn't been busy chipping through the arctic circle of my mother's freezer to remove Tater Tots that expired twenty years ago."

Fi swallowed a spoonful of yogurt and made a dismayed face. "You need to diversify your palate," she said, and handed me my own yogurt. "That man today, if he was any real trouble, would have done something when you were inside. The element of surprise is gone, so now they—whoever they are—must know you're looking for them."

"Or they don't think anything at all," I said.

Most people that get hired to intimidate other people aren't exactly deep thinkers. If they were, they'd find another line of work. People who are hired to watch other people and get spotted immediately are even worse off—if you're not proficient at sitting and staring, it likely means you have no training. Spies learn to watch not from a hiding place, but from a place where others aren't likely to actually be looking. Sitting in a hundred-thousand-dollar car across the street from someone's house isn't exactly Langley training.

"When did Dinino check in?" I asked.

"Same day as Gennaro," Sam said.

"Any idea where he was when we were in the hotel?"

"No," Sam said. "But I have a buddy who might be able to find out." Sam opened up another window on his computer and typed Nicholas

Dinino's name into Google's Blog Search engine, and five seconds later we were looking at the society blog for *Palm Life* magazine, a local rag that covered the glamorous life in Miami, which typically meant they took a lot of photos of wealthy people trying to look casual. It didn't really work, since it's hard to look casual with an entire diamond mine on your body.

It's nearly impossible to move about the world undetected if you're the least bit famous. Anyone with a cell phone is seconds away from telling anyone who is interested—or completely uninterested, for that matter—your precise location. In this case, the *Palm Life* blog was one of just ten blogs that had photos of Dinino from the previous evening. It helped that he posed with a lot of actors, musicians, models and the professionally famous.

On *Palm Life*'s page, Dinino was squished between a rap music impresario, his girl-group girlfriend and the host of one of those shows on cable where chefs try to win prizes for being really great chefs. Just off in the back of the frame were two guys who looked rather odd contextually, since they were wearing black suits that clearly covered guns while everyone else was wearing all white. Shoes, shirts, pants, hats, gloves.

"Labor Day can't come soon enough," Fiona said.

"Says here it's an annual party they have," Sam said.

"Just because it happens every year doesn't mean it's a good idea," Fiona said. "The locusts used to come every year, too."

Regardless of attire, Dinino didn't look in the least bit concerned, though the security in the back did indicate that he was aware enough to bring his own muscle, if indeed they were his.

"These guys look familiar?" I said to Sam, hoping maybe he'd seen them this morning.

"I dunno, Mikey. The guys guarding Bonaventura's place looked like they'd done a lot of Green Side–type work," Sam said. "These men look like bodybuilders." Green Side operations typically involve locating the enemy, watching the enemy and then figuring out how to kill them without getting noticed. Green Side ops could hide in your yogurt and you wouldn't know it until you were chewing on their heads.

It helps that Green Side ops are often covered in camouflage while crawling through a bog during the middle of the night.

I've always preferred a suit. But jeans are nice. A T-shirt is very functional.

When you wear jeans and a T-shirt, there's less chance of finishing a job and finding leeches attached to your thighs, because when you're in the real world, where there aren't a lot of bogs or a pressing need to crawl, jeans and T-shirts train you to be inconspicuous. If you look like a spy, people are going to notice you.

Sam spotted Bonaventura's men immediately because they were a visible deterrent with trademark training and weaponry.

Spies don't wear tuxedos every day. They don't order the same drinks in every city—shaken, stirred or otherwise—and don't leave a trail of bodies in their wake.

You're a spy because you're good at doing the things no one wants to see, and doing it in such a way that no one notices.

Men like those watching Dinino, and the one at my mother's house that morning, aren't smart enough to blend in or avoid the cameras. Which means they aren't professionals, just people who've been hired.

"We're grasping at straws here," I said. "Gennaro's wife and daughter are trapped somewhere in the Atlantic and we need to figure out why. Sam, we need to find out which room at the hotel, other than Gennaro's, is viewing that Web site."

"Got it, Mikey."

"And, Fi, I need you to find out who was driving one of Timothy Sherman's rentals today."

Fi exhaled dramatically. "I hope I don't end up accidentally beating the information out of Mr. Sherman," she said.

"Try your best," I said.

"And where are you going to be?" Fiona asked.

When you want to avoid being ambushed, either by forces or information, the best thing to do is engage first. You might not know the level of resistance you're apt to find, but you'll have the advantage of nuance since you already know the logic of the enemy: They aren't bold enough to strike you head-on, so they think they have to surprise you from the side, cloaked in cover.

"I'm going to be controlling the flow of information," I said.

8

Most of the time, spy work isn't about uncovering what's hidden, but interpreting what is in plain sight. The majority of intelligence information isn't gleaned from men in frogman suits breaking into underwater lairs, but from men in suits reading blogs, newspapers, open-source documents like financial reports, and missives from the men and women stationed in embassies around the world. What might be useless data to you becomes intelligence by virtue of the person reading it.

Expertise creates usable intelligence.

That means you need to know how to find intelligence that doesn't actually exist, which Sam was doing. And sometimes you need to create intelligence, which is what I was doing going with Gennaro to Christopher Bonaventura's vacation home.

And why? First, I called and asked my brother Nate to come, too.

"What's my take on this?" Nate asked.

"Karma," I said.

"You can't eat karma," Nate said. "I can't tell the power company that the karma is in the mail."

I was pretty sure Nate was actually stealing his electricity, but decided to let that fact go. "I'm just asking you to go somewhere and stand silently by my side," I said. I'd tell him later that *somewhere* meant "a mafioso's compound." If I told him ahead of time, he'd be far too willing to help.

"Do I get to carry?"

"Yes," I said. The truth was that he had to be carrying a gun. If he wasn't, it just wouldn't look right for what I was planning.

"Loaded?"

"Loaded. Safety off. You can even use one of my silencers if you like. All I ask is that you put on a suit, that you do what I tell you and that you don't speak. Not a single word."

"Do you have a color preference on the suit, Mr. Westen?"

The nice thing about Nate, in situations like this, is that he's actually pretty handy with a gun and can help out if things get really difficult. He can punch. He can bite. He can kick people in the groin. He has all the moves, if not any of the actual skill or precision. And I can trust him. The bad thing about Nate, in situations like this, is that he's still Nate.

"Whatever you want, Nate," I said, but then thought better of it, lest he actually wear whatever he wanted. "Anything but white. And wear a tie."

I told him to pick us up from the Setai in two hours.

"I think you're forgetting something."

It was true. I was forgetting lots of things. Forgetting the time when we were kids and he thought it would be funny to set the fire station on fire. Forgetting the time he threw a phone book at my head. Forgetting the times I've done jobs for him that invariably involved me nearly getting killed by Russian crime syndicates.

"Why don't you enlighten me," I said.

"A thank-you would be nice," he said.

Ma.

"Oh, right, sorry, Nate," I said. "I owe you for yesterday."

"And the last decade or so."

"I appreciate it," I said.

"Good. Your half of the flowers was fifty dollars. Times that by ten years and I'll call it even for standing around silently for you today," he said, and hung up.

I apprised Nate of the situation at hand while he drove his limo from the hotel to Key Biscayne. I was going to let Christopher Bonaventura know that Gennaro was working with us and that his sporting interests were now over.

"What's my name?" Nate asked.

"How about Nate?" I said.

"That's not working. If I'm going to be some

henchman, I need a henchman name. Three-Finger Frank or something."

"You understand that Mafia guys get their names from their actions or physical descriptions, right? It's not some arbitrary name to scare people."

"Yeah?"

"So if you want me to call yourself Three-Finger Frank," I said, "you're going to need to lose some fingers."

Nate went silent. I looked in the rearview mirror to see how Gennaro was handling this. He looked stricken.

"This is going to work out fine, Gennaro," I said. "Just do what I say and we'll have one problem eliminated."

"You don't know Christopher," Gennaro said.

"I know people much worse than him," I said. Gennaro shook his head slightly, like he was trying to move things around in it until they made sense again.

My plan was simple, which was perhaps why Gennaro seemed so grave: tell Bonaventura that Gennaro was now in my pocket and that if he had any side business with him, aware or otherwise, it would have to come through me, too. Three things could come from this:

1. Bonaventura would agree and then try to have me killed.

2. Bonaventura would disagree and then try to have me killed.
3. Bonaventura would ask to go into business with me, I'd agree, and then he'd probably try to have me killed.

What I knew without a doubt, however, was that he wouldn't kill me right where I stood, particularly not with Gennaro standing beside me. And by the time he did decide to kill me, we'd have figured out the root system here, which likely would mean that Christopher Bonaventura would have larger problems.

"When I was in school," Gennaro said, "Christopher protected me. Someone came at me, he dealt with them. Maybe he just feels like he's still helping me, even if I don't want the help."

"This isn't high school," I said. "And I have to think that if Christopher is now all about the altruism, he wouldn't have blown up that yacht yesterday."

We were already on Key Biscayne at this point and the cars surrounding us in traffic were filled with people driving back home from work, kids getting picked up from day care, families heading off to dinner.

When you see Miami on television, it's always bikinis and diamonds and flashy cars. It's cops and crooks and bags of cocaine. But in real life, people actually live in Miami, raise families, work nine to five, and try to give normal life a go.

Regular people.

Regular cars.

Regular problems.

It seemed like a long time since my problems—and the problems of the people I encountered—weren't literally life-and-death.

It was also a million miles away from Gennaro Stefania's situation. Here was a man whose wife and child we're kidnapped and no one knew, not even the wife and child.

"I just don't understand any of this," Gennaro said.

"You have any idea why your stepfather would want to see Maria dead?" I asked.

"Maria? No. No. He adores her. He adores Liz. He wants for nothing."

"What do you think he was doing meeting with Christopher?"

Gennaro shook his head. "I don't know," he said. "They are familiar with each other, but if we were in Italy he wouldn't be seen within a hundred miles of him. The paparazzi would devour him for it."

There was something else. Something Gennaro didn't know. Something, hopefully, we'd find out after Sam got done at the hotel, where he was busy putting eyes and ears on Dinino's Internet activities.

"Maybe it's nothing," I said. I was trying to

sound hopeful, and for a few seconds of silence, maybe it worked.

And then Nate said, "How about Slade?" as if we were still talking about the slate of imaginary names he was considering. Which, apparently, to him, we were.

"You want me to call you *Slade*?"

"What's wrong with that?"

"What's right with that?"

"Look," Nate said, "if I'm going into this, I gotta know who I am. Strong, silent, cool, I'm with that. But if I need to flex, I should have a name at the ready. What if I get captured? You want me to just blurt out my name and address and social security number?"

Flex? At some point, Nate started picking up words from gangster rap and movies where people turn their guns sideways to shoot each other.

"We're not invading Iran," I said. "No one is going to capture you."

"What's your cover?"

Sam had a buddy of his dummy up some street credentials for me—which means, essentially, if anyone goes looking for information on Tommy the Ice Pick, they're likely to hear he's Las Vegas mafia with Chicago backing. The Sicilians think of the American mafia, if they're not from the original five families, like perpetual rookies. For someone like Bonaventura, the mere idea of checking me out would be admitting that he'd lost a notch.

"Tommy," I said.

"Just Tommy?"

I didn't want to tell Nate about the Ice Pick part and I didn't really want Gennaro to hear it, either. He was already sweating.

"From Vegas."

"Tommy from Vegas?"

"Right," I said.

"So we're in from Las Vegas. Muscling into this action. Getting our piece." Nate was near giddy.

I turned around and looked at Gennaro. "It's going to be fine," I said. "He won't be speaking."

It was just after five when we pulled up to Bonaventura's gate. There were still a good half-dozen men on the other side of it. When they saw us pull up, they opened the gate and one of the men walked up to the car and tapped on the driver's window.

"You're at the wrong place," the man said. Sam was right: He looked like a Marine. Even the way he was standing, like he was trying to figure out how to kick down the door of the limo and start shooting.

Surprisingly, Nate just stared forward and didn't speak.

"I got Gennaro Stefania in the back to see the big guy," I said. I was staring forward, too. Just a profile with sunglasses.

The man craned his head into the car and made out Gennaro in the back.

"You weren't expected today, Mr. Stefania," he said.

"I didn't know I was coming," Gennaro said, just as I told him to say. Whatever questions anyone had, his answer was the same: He didn't know.

"I can let you in," the man said, "but your detail has to stay out here. That's orders."

"We're not his *detail*," I said. "You tell the big guy that Tommy the Ice Pick is out here, and either he lets us in with Mr. Stefania or we start removing Mr. Stefania's nonvital organs." I pulled my sunglasses down and turned to face the guard. Let him see my face. Let him see my eyes. Let him know I wasn't scared in the least. "You know what the spleen does, Jarhead? Does it have an actual purpose? Because that's the only *detail* you might want to consider."

The guard kept his eyes on me but didn't show any emotion. "One moment," he said, and walked back through the gate, shutting it behind him.

"Tommy the Ice Pick?" Nate said.

"Tommy Two Toes doesn't exactly scare people," I said. The guards were clustered behind the gate now and were checking their guns and readjusting their Kevlar.

Not a good sign.

"Is this going to work?" Gennaro said.

"Yes," I said.

"What's the protocol if they start shooting?" Nate said.

"They're not going to start shooting," I said. Though I wasn't 100 percent certain of that declaration, it seemed reasonable to me that a firefight on the most expensive street in Key Biscayne would probably bring the kind of bad publicity people tend to shun, even people like Christopher Bonaventura, at least while on American soil.

Jarhead stepped away from the group and talked into his Bluetooth for a moment. He nodded twice. He turned and stared at the car. From his facial expressions, you'd think he was trying to decide whether he wanted a latte or a mocha. I could tell he was concentrating, but that he was also assessing the entire situation going on around him.

This was not his most difficult experience involving cars, men and guns. You could almost see him standing in Kabul at a roadblock. The funny thing is that I had the odd sense that I *had* seen him in Kabul.

Not funny like it was amusing, but funny like I was starting to wonder if I was walking into something much larger than myself.

A few moments later, Jarhead stepped back through the gate and stood by Nate's window. "Thank you for your patience," he said, his voice flat; friendly even. He looked from Nate to me— maybe a moment longer on me—and then back toward Gennaro. Made eye contact with each of us, let us know he was in control of the situation. "Mr. Bonaventura would be happy to meet any friends of Mr. Stefania's. However, you pull through this gate and make a single move I determine to be threatening? We will light you the fuck up. We understand?"

I had to hand it to Jarhead. He knew how to play the game. "That's what I like to hear!" I pounded my hands on the dashboard. "You get tired of this yes-man shit, you got a job with Tommy the Ice Pick, Jarhead." His eyes flickered slightly. Either he didn't like being called Jarhead or he was silently filing away my name. Either way was fine with me. "Let me correct myself: *Mr.* Jarhead," I said, and put up my hands. "No disrespect. Don't light us the fuck up, okay?"

Jarhead didn't say another word. He just stepped away from the window and waved open the gates.

"Nice guy," Nate said after he put his window back up.

"That's why I don't want you talking," I said.

Surprisingly, Nate didn't argue the point. Maybe it was because we were pulling past the phalanx of guards, each of whom looked at us with nothing short of boredom in their eyes, which was a touch disconcerting since they had their guns pointed at us, too. Jarhead and two other men followed behind us in a golf cart.

"I didn't think the Mafia hired out," Nate said.

"It's a recent development," I said.

If you're a decent crime boss, invested in staying a crime boss who rules from a mansion, not a prison cell, you take note of changes in law enforcement. It used to be easy to kill off your competition by bashing them to death with a phone and then burying them in a field somewhere or tossing them into a river.

That was before DNA testing and the advent of forensic crime scene investigation.

Beat someone to death with a phone and you're going to leave a million clues for investigators, everything from skin cells to hair fibers to microscopic bits of plastic that contain their own fingerprints from their production cycle. Hit someone on the back of the head with an old rotary-dial phone and forensic experts will be able to trace one slice of plastic molding all the way back to the day it was poured.

Beat someone with your fists and you might as well just leave your social security number on the body, too.

Likewise, if you dig a grave in a cornfield, you're going to leave footprints and fingerprints and hair follicles and skin cells from your car all the way to the grave, and unless you're wearing a hazmat suit, there's an excellent chance you'll drop fibers from your car, your home, your victim's clothing and your Doberman's chew toy along with it all.

If you want to kill someone these days and want to avoid capture, you hire a professional.

Not a hit man.

A professional. Trained by the government in espionage and assassination. A person who not only knows how to kill but knows how not to leave evidence or, better, only leave evidence that points in the direction you want it to point. When investigations consisted only of a detective pounding on doors, you could afford to be brazen—pay off enough people above him and it wouldn't matter what he found.

But today you'd need to pay off scientists in the basement of a university maybe five hundred miles away. You'd have to know what every single piece of evidence was to figure out which labs were being used.

You'd need to pay off a blood-spatter expert.

A biologist.

A chemical engineer.

The evidence chain used to go between one or two people. Now it's more like a hundred.

Mafia bosses don't get away with murder anymore because they're criminal masterminds or are able to act above the law by virtue of their payoffs; they get away because they understand the science of investigation and how to kill someone in a clean environment. Or if they don't, they hire people who do.

As we pulled up the expansive drive, I noticed that in addition to the men there were also the armor-plated cars Sam mentioned, the bikes and, to my surprise and delight, running around the vast acreage to the east of the house, about twenty children with balloons. I also made out a clown, a small elephant with a child on its back being guided around the circumference of the property and tables covered in presents, food and pyramids of glasses. There were a few older women sitting in lawn chairs and other younger women milling about with the children and lingering near the tables of food. Under a white tent there were a dozen tables being set up, and a series of cooking stations were being arranged along the back of the room. There were pink and white streamers everywhere, including one huge one strung across the front of the tent that said HAPPY 5TH BIRTHDAY, TINA!

"We grew up in the wrong part of town," Nate said.

"I'm not so sure," I said.

"Did I even have a fifth birthday?"

I told him I thought we went to Red Vest Pizza, a place our father liked to go to on account of the dollar beers. "There wasn't a pachyderm in sight, if you're curious," I said. "Who is Tina?" I asked Gennaro.

"Christopher's daughter."

This new information—the party—required a distinct change in thought.

"Gennaro," I said, "if at some point during this meeting it looks like there's going to be a fight, just know that I'm not going to let anyone hurt you. Okay?"

"What?" Gennaro said, now in full panic.

"When was the last time you were in a fight?"

"Never," he said.

"Not once?"

"I told you, Christopher protected me when we were kids, and these days I have people like you."

People like me. Great.

"If it looks like a situation where you might find yourself in a compromised position, I'll hit you first. If I have to hit you, just know you probably won't remember it." This didn't ease Gennaro's panic. "But it probably won't come to that, really. So just be calm."

I actually wanted Gennaro slightly uneasy, as if he were really being yanked about by someone like Tommy the Ice Pick.

Christopher Bonaventura was in the Mafia.

Tommy the Ice Pick was in the mob.

The difference is that a person like Tommy the Ice Pick would actually kill you with his own hands. Christopher Bonaventura was more about outsourcing.

"And, Nate, don't do anything, okay? I don't want you getting hurt, either. These guys aren't thugs, they're actual professionals. Something happens to me that I can't control, you're not going to control it, either."

"Then why am I here?"

"In case I *need* you to do something. And in that case, make it happen."

That got Nate smiling. There's a part of Nate's reptilian brain that responds well to conversations that essentially state the obvious but in ways you might hear in old Clint Eastwood movies.

Nate parked the limo next to one of the black Suburbans, and by the time we stepped out Jarhead and the other two men were already waiting for us. Their guns were out of sight, but I figured Jarhead for the kind of guy who would prefer to stick his KA-BAR into your kidneys.

"Mr. Bonaventura is inside," Jarhead said, as we walked toward the front of the mansion. Nate and Gennaro were just in front of me, the two other guards at their flanks. "He can give you ten minutes. Minute eleven and you're back in your car. There is no negotiation."

"If we get out in five," I said, "you think I could get a slice of cake to go?"

"We get inside," Jarhead said, "and you act like a gentleman and give me whatever you have on your leg, whatever you have on your back and anything else you think I might want. Minute eleven, you get it all back."

"Yeah, and what's in it for me?" I said.

Jarhead smiled. It wasn't menacing. It wasn't mocking. It wasn't even an inadvertent twitching of the facial muscles. It looked like Jarhead was actually happy about something. "Your meeting goes off without a hitch," he said, "Mr. Stefania and your silent friend get out alive, and I don't tell Mr. Bonaventura that I know you."

Jarhead stepped in front of me before I could answer him and opened the front door of the house into a foyer inlaid with marble. Inside, a steady stream of people moved back and forth with huge platters of food held head high. A small gold dog scurried about and barked.

One thing for certain, no one was getting shot today. Not Gennaro. Not Nate. Not me. But that didn't make any of this good news. If Jarhead knew me, he knew a lot more, too. That he wasn't acting on this knowledge told me that I was staring at someone who knew my file, someone who knew the truth, someone who knew that I was Michael Westen, and that Michael Westen was not someone he really wanted to engage in front of school children, women and one very large land mammal.

It meant that no matter who I pretended to be, whatever ruse I perpetrated, I had to offer some nugget of truth that would keep the situation in my favor, so that Jarhead would understand that this game belonged to me, even if I wasn't entirely clear what we were playing.

Or whom.

9

The careful art of subversion involves turning people against their own leaders. During a long campaign, this entails intricate—and intimate—psychological warfare mixed with a fair amount of propaganda. This means everything from arming opposition leaders to facilitating the escape of political prisoners to simply attending to the core needs of the people you wish to convert.

You give them money and prescription drugs.

You pave their roads.

You give children candy and toys.

And then you tell the people that their government is corrupt and controlled by a puppet master in the west, the east, the north, the south.

And if none of that works? You capture them, torture them, tell them they have two choices: Join your militia or die.

Most people will opt to live.

Sometimes, this all works our perfectly. . . . And most everyone dies, regardless.

Guatemala.

Cuba.

Iraq.

Iraq again.

That knowledge gave me pause.

Telling someone that you know they are lying—and lying to their leader—and yet refusing to act is one of the basest forms of subversion. You do it to build trust while creating a false sense of reciprocal empathy between a rank-and-file soldier just doing his job and the person they are charged with guarding.

But if Jarhead knew who I was, that meant he was aware of one of the most profound truths concerning intelligence: You can't bullshit a bullshitter.

So as Jarhead directed us through the house, I broke him down from the available information, which was only what I could see, what Sam had told me, and what I had to assume.

He was:

A Marine. Probably Force Recon, which meant he'd spent the last several years in combat situations requiring far more mental acuity than walking uninvited guests to a sitting room.

A trained killer. The difference between a trained killer and a psychopath is usually distance. A trained killer shoots at objects at the end of a scope and can marginalize them into "kills" without considering that human element. The targets are impediments to freedom, or the crossing of a bridge or the clearing of a hot zone. Force Recon Marines, however, tend to recruit men not morally opposed to close fighting—whites-of-their-eyes moments—if the need arises. But there's not a lot of close fighting when you have Apaches and Black Hawks on your team, too.

Psychopaths prefer to cut you into bite-sized pieces using their nail clippers.

An American. This was important, particularly since he was an American working for an Italian crime boss. You commit a crime in America involving a gun and, provided you are apprehended and convicted, you're looking at between five and twenty years of prison time, but the truth is that if you have a decent lawyer and a relatively clean record and are a war hero, you're probably on the street in six months.

Commit a crime with a gun in the service of a foreign national involved in criminal enterprise on American soil, and you're looking at federal time. Do it as an American soldier and there's a good chance they'll try you for treason.

All of this worked in our theoretical favor.

There was also a pretty good chance that Jarhead had already played out these issues in his own mind, too, and didn't care.

Nihilism is always a wild card.

Jarhead stopped before the open doors of a sitting room that overlooked the water. The walls were covered in bookshelves and surrounded two couches that faced each other in the center of the room. A mahogany coffee table was placed between the couches, and as we entered the room a woman was placing a tray of ice water and lemonade onto it, along with several glasses and a plate of cookies.

Nate started to move toward the food—it might have just been reflex on his part—but I grabbed his arm and pulled him back.

It's important to appear courteous and hospitable when dealing with your enemies. It's more important to make sure they eat first, not just out of custom, but to ensure the food isn't poisoned.

When the woman left, Jarhead finally spoke again. "Please give me all of your weapons," he said. Usually in a situation like this, I'd be concerned that Nate might do something stupid, like start shooting, but I'd made my calculations and felt somewhat secure that Jarhead was working on the level—or at least a level that allowed him to be threatening, but not outright murderous—so I immediately began disarming and handing everything over to one of Jarhead's men, which caused Nate to do the same thing.

Jarhead hadn't said another word directly to me, but I was certain now that when he said he knew me, he wasn't speaking philosophically. Now I was trying to figure out how.

My first impression upon seeing him was that he'd been in Kabul. The truth, however, is that he could have been anywhere. We could have huddled against a berm together for five minutes in Iraq. We could have been in a classroom in Virginia. We could have sat next to each other on an Apache hovering over Malawi.

What was obvious, no matter the situation, was that he didn't know Tommy the Ice Pick and wasn't all that concerned by my deception. At least not to the point that he actually acted on his knowledge, which in and of itself was cause for concern.

There's subversion and then there's third-rail treachery. Jarhead was standing close enough to the latter to be putting off sparks, playing both sides without any visible recompense.

Which meant he had his own agenda, provided I didn't try to choke Christopher Bonaventura to death.

"You ever do any time?" I said to Jarhead once all of the guns were collected. "Because you look like a guy I knew back in the day."

"Worked in the post office for a little while," Jarhead said flatly.

This was good.

We were now officially speaking in code.

When you're a spy or an operative like Jarhead, working in the post office means you've been disseminating propaganda and doing incursions into foreign countries.

In the early days of Vietnam, this meant sending CIA operatives into the country as journalists and aid workers who could alter the news, ferment change via small-group discussions in hamlets and villages and salt any open wounds helpful to American concerns.

And occasionally executing people.

In Iraq and Afghanistan, it was more of the same, but a higher reliance on executing people and *then* altering the news, leafleting hamlets and then, if need be, engaging in blackmail, extortion and general malfeasance, all under the guise of democratic nation building.

Freedom has certain responsibilities, and very few of them are pretty if you happen to be standing on foreign soil and prefer a more totalitarian ruling technique.

"I don't get a lot of mail," I said. "I'm sort of an off-the-grid kinda guy, know what I'm saying? You ever live in the East?"

"Worked out there," he said. "Went to school up North."

Translation: was stationed in the Middle East, or at least dropped in a few times in the dead of night and took out Baath party members in advance of a Humvee line. Trained in North Africa, which meant we had similar skill sets.

Not a great development.

"You get to any clubs? Maybe I seen you at one?"

"Didn't go out much after I stopped working at

the post office," he said. "Just wanted to stay home. And now I get to make my own hours. But who knows? Something interesting happens in the mail industry, maybe I'll get back into it. I just love to work."

Translation?

Covert Ops.

Decommissioned.

Freelance.

Loves to answer the phone at three a.m., put on black body armor and kill people.

Further translation:

No problem killing my entire family, if that's what his orders were.

"Great," I said. "Good you like your job."

We stared at each other for a few seconds, each of us taking account.

There weren't a lot of soft spots on Jarhead. My best chance with him would be to go for his eyes, try to get knuckle deep in one and see if he submitted, which was unlikely. Jarhead didn't look like the kind of guy who submitted to anything.

Likewise, Jarhead was trying to calculate my soft spot. He looked me up and down slightly and then, almost imperceptibly, cut his gaze to Nate.

"Working with family is more rewarding," he said. "I learned that from Mr. Bonaventura."

He was good. And he knew it.

Happy with his progress in sussing out the threat level in the room, Jarhead told one of his men to get the boss, and a few moments later Christopher Bonaventura stepped into the room with a studied nonchalance.

In photos, Bonaventura looks dapper and collected, like he's always about to sip a martini and smoke a cigar before engaging in a lively game of chance somewhere in Monaco, just prior to jumping on a Learjet bound for the Caymans.

Or ordering the murder of his father, because the truth is that he is a thug. Nothing more. Nothing less.

But on this day, he was a thug holding a birthday party for the five-year-old daughter, which meant he wasn't looking terribly dapper. He had on a plain white T-shirt, tan shorts that showed off his pale knees, and I noticed that he hadn't bothered to put on any shoes. There were bits of grass and dirt between his toes, and he smelled vaguely like cotton candy, which made sense since there were tiny pink gobs of it on his chin.

Bonaventura looked around the room, shrugged once, sat down on one of the couches, poured himself a glass of lemonade, drank it, wiped his mouth off with the back of his hand, and then turned to me and said, "Who the fuck are you?" His accent was prominent, but he'd been educated in America and spent enough time here to have a library stocked with books in English. It seemed like he was a big Harry Potter fan, but maybe that was for his kid.

"Tommy Feraci," I said. I extended a hand towards him but he didn't move. "From Las Vegas originally, but now I'm cohabitating in these here parts." I pointed at Nate. "That's my man Slade." I pointed at Gennaro. "That's your mark."

"You know this guy, Gennaro?" Gennaro said he did. Bonaventura took another sip of his lemonade, swallowed, seemed to contemplate the information he had and then said, "You have some sort of business proposal for me, is that right?"

"Not so much a proposal," I said. "I don't propose. This is more like an infomercial. I'm gonna tell you what's what and then you tell me how much you're buying."

Christopher Bonaventura burst out laughing. He laughed until it became uncomfortable for the rest of us standing and watching him, so I sat down across from him, poured myself a glass of lemonade, too, and waited for him to calm down, which he did directly.

"I like you," Bonaventura said. "You come to my home, during my daughter's birthday, you bring my old friend Gennaro with you like a captive and then you tell me how it's going to be. You don't need my permission Tommy. Go about your business with Gennaro with my blessing. That's how much I like you. None of my business."

"I think that's where we aren't seeing things correctly. My business with Gennaro directly relates to your business with Gennaro."

"I'm not in business with Gennaro," he said. "Are we, Gennaro?"

"I don't know what to think," Gennaro said.

"You leave that up to your wife now, too?" Bonaventura said. "First she tells you who you can be friends with, and now she tells you what to think? Your father would be ashamed of you."

Gennaro flinched but didn't say anything.

"Here's the dilly-o," I said, ignoring whatever was going on between the two of them. And by *ignoring*, I mean that I was paying absolute attention, but that Tommy the Ice Pick had a single-minded determination to get on with the conversation. "I can't have you working the open seas like you're Gaspar. This is my water, so you won't be fixing races on it unless I say so."

"Gennaro, why would you tell him I'm doing that?"

Gennaro looked at me and then back at Bonaventura. If he followed the script, we'd be fine. "He has my wife and child," Gennaro said. "He told me if I don't lose the race he'll kill them and then me."

Perfect.

"Here's how it is," I said. I motioned to Nate, who was holding up a bookcase with his back while trying to look menacing. "My guy Slade over there takes a lot of action on these races, and everyone he talked to this week said the *Pax Bellicosa* was the way to go. Lots of cheese going that direction. So I made a couple calls. Talked to some guys on the other boats—and by talk, I think you know what I'm saying, right, Chrissy?—and it all came back to you."

"If this were true," he said, "why would it be any concern of yours? Where did you say you're from?"

"Las Vegas originally. Spent a couple years in Angola—the one in Louisiana—and finished up down here at Glades, and my friends have been nice enough to let me set up my own shop here. Guess I just got used to the clean Florida life," I said. "See, no disrespect, but this race isn't being held in Corfu, so you want to get into this in Miami, you go through my shop. And then there's the issue that my shop has certain worldwide interests involving Mr. Stefania here, and they don't involve him winning any more races."

Bonaventura stood up and walked over to the window. He was still sipping on his lemonade. Perfectly casual. Not a single ounce of stress in his bones. "You seem like a reasonable person, Tommy."

"That's what people say," I said.

"And I think I'm a reasonable person. Wouldn't you say that, Gennaro? That people consider me reasonable above all else?"

"I don't know," Gennaro said.

"Sure you do," Bonaventura said. "Wasn't I *reasonable* when you came to me for help? Wasn't I *reasonable* in not telling your family of your own insecurities? Wasn't I *reasonable* when we were kids, Gennaro? Didn't I handle all of your problems then in a *reasonable* way?"

I didn't like where this was going.

"Hey, everybody thinks everybody is a peach, right?" I said.

"Right," Bonaventura said. "So let's do a little algebra, Tommy. Is the water in . . . what did you say, Corfu? . . . is that the same water that flows through this bay?"

"Hey," I said, "I ain't some kinda waterologist here. You want someone to explain to you how water works, go get yourself a dolphin. You want to know how money works, we can talk." I was walking a very thin line between cocky and the victim of an assassination, though I thought it was unlikely Jarhead would do anything to me. If he knew who I was, he knew what I was capable of, and I was capable of taking down this entire room in less than a minute, though when I looked over at Jarhead again I did some quick math and decided it would probably take an extra forty seconds or so to deal with him. Thing was, right when I looked over at Jarhead he looked right at me, as if maybe he was doing the same math. "No disrespect," I continued, "but this isn't bocce ball we're talking about here."

Bonaventura laughed again. "You pretend that you're dumb, Tommy," he said. He walked back across the room and stood directly in front of me, so that I had to look up at him from my spot on the sofa. I could see the smoothness of his skin up close, could smell his cologne, could see the glint of diamonds off his watch.

Could break both of his legs in fifteen seconds.

Maybe less.

"But I know you're smart," he said, and then pointed a finger at me, but not in a threatening way. Just pointing out the obvious. "So I'm going to explain to you one time the universal truth of this business you think you're in. All the water that I see is mine. I don't care where in the world I am—if I want it, it's mine. If I choose to have sway over a race in Miami, or in Italy, or in the fucking toilet you sit on each morning, I do it. There is no why. I do it. So you tell your people to leave his family alone, or you, your people, everyone your people know, have a problem. Do we understand?"

"I don't know who *we* are," I said. I spread my legs out so Bonaventura was actually in the V between my feet, effectively trapping him where he stood. "But I know I understand one thing, and you told me another."

"Your smugness is not becoming and it will not last," Bonaventura said. He looked down and saw my legs. "If you'll excuse me, I have a birthday party to get back to."

If you were a lunatic, this would be the moment when you would kick Christopher Bonaventura in the knees, and then while he was down you'd probably kick him in the head, too. You'd stand on top of him and you'd say something you first heard on television or in a music video or uttered by an action hero. . . . And then Jarhead would shoot you in the back of your skull.

Tommy the Ice Pick was a lunatic.

Michael Westen didn't want to get shot in the back of the head.

But neither of us was letting him go yet.

"Out of curiosity," I said, "where do you get an elephant? My kid, she's always asking for a puppy or a gerbil, and I figure one day, who knows, I might pick one up. But you can't just go into PetSmart and find yourself an elephant, am I right?"

"Move your legs," Bonaventura said.

"I'm not done talking to you yet," I said. "I'm not some punk you can just brush off. I've got people ready to kill your friend Gennaro's wife if things don't go as I want them to go. Show him your phone, G."

Gennaro dug his phone from his pocket and handed it to Bonaventura, who looked at the video for a moment and handed it back without a word.

I couldn't tell if he was surprised or not. So I explained it to him; see if he blinked. He showed nothing, so I went on. "You want that I kill Maria and make poor Liz watch? You want that on your plate? Because the first person the FBI and cops and Interpol look to isn't going to be Tommy

Feraci. It's going to be you, Chrissy. You think the FBI isn't going to find out you've been fixing his races? That's some RICO shit right there, partner, and it's a lot easier to prove than mail fraud."

"You have nothing," Bonaventura said. "They have nothing."

"No, they had nothing on Capone. You know where he ended up? Right here in Miami, brain sick from the syphilis. Ended up dead in his big-ass mansion over on Palm Island. You can probably see his place out your window, right there on *your* water. Me? I got your friend Gennaro here," I said. "I got every single person my guy Slade put an ounce of pressure on, each rolled on you like it was their job, like if they rolled on you, I was gonna give 'em health benefits and a 401(k), you know? Rolled and rolled and rolled, Chrissy. Just one look from Slade was all it took. One look."

Nate straightened up. Flexed his jaw muscles. Sucked in his stomach, puffed out his chest, narrowed his eyes. I'd ask him later where he picked up those moves, since it made him look like he had the stomach flu.

"That's why we're here," I continued. "Just being a *gentleman* about things. Being *reasonable*. You let Gennaro's interests go, or his wife dies, maybe his kid, too, and it's on your ass. Besides, you've made your nut off of this, right? You can absorb a few gambling losses this week, right?"

Taking risks is about calculating the possibility

of success. Hit a 17 against a face card in blackjack and it isn't a risk, it's poor judgment. Telling a mafioso exactly how he would be implicated in the murder of one of the wealthiest women in the world is just good business sense.

Provided the Mafioso isn't already planning the same murder, of course.

That's where the risk came in. I had to hope I was making the right play.

Bonaventura briefly shifted his eyes over to Jarhead. A real bully only attacks when he knows he can't be beaten, when he has someone else to handle his business if it looks like the odds aren't in his favor. And Christopher Bonaventura definitely had the odds.

"You touch Maria Ottone, and you will not sleep another night," Bonaventura said.

A person with actual skill and training doesn't care about the odds, especially when fighting someone who has always relied on personal intimidation and not actual physical prowess in defeating his opponents. . . . Or if the person with skill is actually looking to get hit.

"I wouldn't dream of touching her," I said. "The plan is for one of my guys to chain her to the anchor, toss her over and see if she's Houdini." I looked at my watch. "In about fifteen minutes, if they don't hear from me, Gennaro's wife will be under *your* water, Chrissy."

If you want to avoid getting hit in the face and

aren't much of a fighter, the best thing to do is run away. Adrenaline and fear will give you a burst of speed that your attacker may not be able to match. It will also give you the opportunity to find a weapon or, better, other people. Civil society is usually more of a deterrent to violence than a piece of balsa wood being waved by someone in mortal fear for their life.

If running isn't an option, you want to control the situation as best as you can. That means controlling the point of attack. If you're going to get hit in the face—if, in fact, you're encouraging someone to hit you in the face—the forehead is the best possible landing position for their fist.

The forehead's main job is to protect your brain, which makes it one of the hardest plates in the human body. As a side benefit, your forehead has an interstate of thick blood vessels crisscrossing from just above your eyebrows up through your hairline, and, when punctured, they tend to geyser. It's how every professional wrestler is able to bleed out on the mat and still make it back into the ring the next weekend.

Most people not involved in professional wrestling don't care for the sight of blood, particularly not blood in geyser form.

The other side benefit is that there's a pretty good chance that the person hitting you in the forehead is going to break his hand or at least a few fingers or knuckles, especially if you're someone like Christopher Bonaventura, who'd just tucked his thumb into his fist; it's a common tactic seen in five-year-old girls and nervous Mafia bosses who realize they've been backed into a corner by someone calling himself Tommy the Ice Pick.

So as Christopher Bonaventura swung down at me, I tilted my head back and thrust my neck upward, letting him catch me flush in the forehead, but without losing any control over my neck muscles.

If you don't want to get knocked out when being hit in the head or face, you have to learn to control the acceleration and deceleration of your head and neck muscles. When someone hits you in the face and you pass out, what's actually happening is that you're having a stroke.

A very small stroke, but a stroke just the same.

You want to avoid having a stroke.

A rotary blow—a roundhouse left, for instance—will cause your head to swivel sharply, compressing and constricting your carotid arteries, which is not a good thing if you enjoy having regular cardiac function or the ability to speak.

An uppercut works in much the same way, except that instead of constricting the carotid, the whiplash effect of the acceleration compresses the circulation to the back of your brain.

Keeping circulation flowing to the back of your brain is important, particularly if you like controlling your motor functions. Getting hit square on the chin might snap your temporomandibular joint like a chicken bone, but if you have strong neck muscles, you'll only pass out from the pain.

If you don't have the opportunity to walk around with weighted headgear for a few hours every day in order to build up muscle, try yoga. The natural resistance training will give you flexibility and core strength. The serenity might keep you away from angry mob bosses intent on punching you in the face.

Barring the ability to achieve any of the above, your only other option is to match or beat the velocity of the object moving toward you, so that when it impacts, most of the damage goes in the other direction.

Or exactly what happened to Christopher Bonaventura's fist.

I felt his thick wedding band dig into the tightened flesh of my forehead, splitting it right where I'd hoped, sending a spray of blood out from my head, which I then flung forward, dousing him, and then dousing the sofa, and getting a few drips and drops on the coffee table, too. If I got the opportunity, I'd walk over to the bookcase and grab *Harry Potter and the Goblet of Fire* and leave a couple streaks there, too. All of which would be hard for Bonaventura to explain to his daughter, the nice invited guests here for her birthday and the elephant tamer, too.

But first he'd need to go to the emergency room,

since as soon as his fist landed on my forehead he
let out a shriek, which told me he'd probably just
broken his thumb, maybe his ring finger, too,
which would serve him right for hitting me with
his wedding band. He stumbled out from between
the sofa and the coffee table, holding his hand and
covered in my blood.

Nate made a move, but Jarhead gave him a
slight shove that sent him back against the wall. It
was a halfhearted effort by both of them, which is
about what I expected. Jarhead was going to let
Bonaventura do what he was going to do, which
didn't end up being much at all, which was
probably better for all involved.

I had two options here: pretend to be really hurt
or be the tough guy.

"That all you got?" I slurred. I staggered up and
then fell back into the sofa.

Bonaventura stood next to Jarhead and glared
at me. It was about all he could muster, since his
hand had already started to balloon grotesquely.
Also, I was shaking my head back and forth,
spreading blood onto as many surfaces as possible. He was going to have quite the cleaning bill,
though something told me he could afford it. His
daughter might only get an alpaca for her next
birthday, however.

"Get this trash out of my home," he said to Jarhead.

"Does that mean we have a deal?" I said. "Because Maria has about ten minutes left on her clock." I tapped my watch. "Tick, tick, tick, Chrissy."

He glared at me some more. The he turned and glared at Gennaro. He took some time doing that glaring thing to everyone in the room, even his own guys. I got the impression that he thought this was a good way of communicating rage and indignation, generally, but at that moment I think it was also a way to keep him from crying out in pain again. "I hope you know what you've done," he said to Gennaro.

"All I know is that I don't want my wife to die," he said. "If I am in this maniac's pocket or yours, I can't see the difference."

Bonaventura walked out of the room without another word, which I took to mean I'd solved one of our problems. I took one of the throw pillows from the sofa and pressed it against my forehead and then stood up, which got the blood flow to stop.

"How many minutes was that?" I said to Jarhead.

"Nine," he said.

"Think I can get a ride on the elephant?"

"Not this time," he said. He motioned to one of his guys, who gave me and Nate back our guns. Jarhead then handed me a card. All it had on it was his name: ALEX KYLE. No number. "Call me," he said. "We should talk."

10

It used to be that the only way you could get reliable information on someone was by tapping his
phone. Get a wire on someone's line and you
could find out the most intimate details of his life.
But now everyone uses e-mail. From a legal
standpoint, it's more difficult to tap into someone's e-mail account than it is to get a wiretap on
his phone.

From an illegal standpoint, it's also harder.

If you want to tap a phone, there are stores in
the mall that will sell you everything you need.
What used to be the most clandestine technology
is now sold as a way of watching your children.
For less than two hundred dollars, you can get the
RDRX-99, a line-activated digital recorder that will
monitor up to five different phone lines at once for
thirty-four hours at a time, and will e-mail you
reports on the time and date of phone calls. If you
don't want to break into someone's home to install

the device in his wall jack, you can always access his outdoor box and place your device there. It requires the same technical precision required to set up a DVD player. Plug A into B and listen.

But if you want to intercept someone's e-mail or track his movements online, it's usually far more complicated.

In a high-level break-in, you'd want to redirect the line of information by locating transmission points—from delivery to reception—and constantly adapt the signal. This means you'd need a very large antenna, expert digital technology that could adjust radio waves and diagnose algorithms, and finally an expert who could decipher it all into a dummy location before letting it through to the actual delivery point, so that the person being tracked wouldn't know anything ill was happening.

If you have an office in Langley or Qatar or even in the Green Zone in Baghdad, you can accomplish this in about an hour's time at a taxpayer cost of about three hundred thousand-dollar staplers.

Or, if you happen to be one wall away from your target, and that target isn't exactly a technical wizard, you can just jam the prevalent Wi-Fi signal using a modified 5.8 GHz cordless telephone, a length of speaker wire and your index finger, and then divert the person you're interested in to your network, which in this case was a powerful Wi-Fi router Sam purchased for the grand total of $77.25 at Staples.

And the result?

"Mikey, the perversion of some people is astounding," Sam said. We were sitting in the Aground Bar at the Southern Cross Yacht Club in Coconut Grove, from where the race would launch in the morning. I'd brought Gennaro over in the Charger after Nate dropped us off, and spent the majority of the ride telling him everything would be fine, that half of his problems were solved.

Not that I actually believed everything was going to be fine just yet, but the odds had improved and I'm an optimist.

Out the window I could see Gennaro and his team working on their yacht. They were due to launch in the bay within the hour to test out the conditions and dry run out into the open sea for several hours in preparation for the race.

Sam had a file open in front of him and was leafing through several sheets of paper.

"What did Dinino have?" I said.

"Well, I'm not specifically talking about Dinino. I had to wait around quite a while until he came back to his room, so I did recon on other folks that seemed suspect, according to, uh, some of their in-room habits."

"I'm shocked," I said.

"I'm just saying," Sam said, "that there's no good reason to ever be searching for a blow-up doll of Alaska's governor. I'm all for privacy, but there have to be limits."

He handed a page over to me. There, in fact, was a blow-up doll of Alaska's governor. It was very lifelike.

"Clearly."

A group of men wearing white slacks and navy blue sport coats with gold buttons and lovely anchors stitched over their breast pockets came and sat at the table beside ours. They regarded Sam and me like we'd just crawled out of a gutter.

"How you fellas doing?" Sam raised his beer at the men, but they didn't respond. "Here for the big race, or do you just love the maritime?"

Nothing.

"Well, nice joint you have here. Any of you guys got any pull with the jukebox? Maybe replace Artie Shaw with something from the last 100 years?"

Nothing.

"All right, then," Sam said, and tipped his beer their direction again. "Avast and Ahoy!"

The Aground normally catered to a clientele of South Florida's richest men, as the Southern Cross Yacht Club didn't admit women into the building, much less the bar, until 1957, and tradition still lingered. They were still largely sexually. segregated, though with *much* charm and aplomb and contemptible politeness, naturally, as the women had a tearoom downstairs where skirts were always required, as if it were still 1957.

And they were certainly socially and economically segregated, too, which was clear when the men got up and moved to another table as one, never once bothering to speak. Maybe it was because the center of my forehead looked like a blood-filled Easter egg. Or maybe it was because we were both in strict violation of the dress code posted above the front door that instructed all patrons in the bar to be in slacks and a coat after four p.m.

"That was subtle," I said.

"Blue bloods have a low tolerance for me." Sam again raised his beer toward the men once they settled at another table. "What can I say? I guess not *everyone* likes me." He slid the rest of the file my way. "Anyway," he said, "Dinino is our guy. He got back to the hotel and within five minutes he was up viewing the site. He sent three e-mails off to the same dummy g-mail address that my buddy Walt routed to Corsica, which is where the person uploading the video is located. How's your Italian?"

"Not bad," I said. I read the e-mails. One was asking when the next video would be uploaded, the second asked for confirmation that proper payment had been received and the third was informing the person in Corsica that their services would no longer be needed after tomorrow. "You get any more of his e-mails?"

"I got in and pulled out everything he's received and sent in the last two weeks," Sam said. "It's all there. You might want to skip to the pictures I printed out. Worth a couple million words, probably several million dollars."

The first photo was of Dinino with a girl of about sixteen. Maybe seventeen. But not any older. They were picking fruit from an open-air market. Looked like Florence.

"Illegitimate daughter?" I said. It was really more of a hope than a true estimation.

"Keep looking," Sam said.

The next series of photos was of Dinino and the girl walking the grounds of the Palazzo Pitti's Boboli Gardens. I flipped through them like the frames of an old cartoon. His hand was in the center of her back and then lower and lower and lower as the photos progressed. The last photo was of them kissing near the entrance to the garden's amphitheater.

"That's not how you kiss your daughter," I said. I tucked the photos back into the file. "Who is she?"

"Jimenez says she's a summer intern in the Ottone offices in Florence," Sam said. "There's a good chance she's a plant."

"This Jimenez fellow is full of great news," I said. "Who planted her?"

"I can tell you who *didn't*," Sam said.

"Please don't say Bonaventura."

"Okay."

Sam took a sip from his beer.

I looked outside. I could make out Gennaro motioning to his crew, stalking along the edge of his boat, giving directions. For whatever it was worth, it looked like he had his mind somewhere else for the first time. I'd removed the fix behind him, as best as I could tell, but his wife and daughter were still out on the sea with nothing stopping their imminent demise.

The blue bloods did their blue-blood thing, which as far as I could tell was to drink Macallan 30 year, neat.

I pondered the bull's-eye on my back from my day's activities with Christopher Bonaventura. Regardless of Dinino's involvement, it was a needed step.

It just never got easier.

"All right," I said. "Tell me."

"It isn't Bonaventura," he said.

"Stunned," I said.

"This afternoon Dinino transferred seventeen thousand in cash advance from a credit card to a bank account in Myanmar." Sam had printed out the screen shot, which showed the account information for the recipient, but no name. "The previous two days he did the same thing. All in, he transferred close to fifty thousand in cash advances from different credit cards."

"You ask your friend Darleen about this?"

Sam either blushed or suddenly had a severe blood flow problem. Whichever was the case, he stopped and took a sip of beer before he answered me and was fully composed by the time the bottle was back on the table. "You get a woman like Darleen on the line," he said, "and you need to play it smooth. Can't just start letting her know you're snooping on people's e-mails."

"I think that's called ethics," I said.

"You ever forget whether or not you had sex with someone?"

"Not that I recall," I said.

"Me either," Sam said. "But if it were to happen, that would be normal, right?"

"Absolutely."

"Anyway," he said, "this bank in Myanmar, it's practically got a flag waving in front of it that says *Drug Dealers Welcome*."

"Then why are you so sure Bonaventura isn't on the other end?" I said.

"It's all Islamic drug money going in there to fund terrorism," Sam said. "Bonaventura might be a killer, but he's a good Catholic, and if he tries to transfer money out of there, he's asking for trouble."

Sam was right. After 9/11, the Patriot Act started designating banks across the world as rogue supporters of terrorism, which meant that if you did business with them, there was a good

chance you'd wake one morning and find someone like me standing at the foot of your bed.

Or not wake up.

And that was if you happened to live in a country that wasn't an American ally. In an allied nation, there was a fair chance that your entire
family would be put on a plane in the middle of
the night and flown to a prison in another foreign
country where you'd be kept as an enemy com-
batant.

And then one day, you might wake up and find
a person like me standing at the foot of your bed
anyway . . . and not to read you your Miranda
rights.

Whoever was getting the transfers didn't care
about those possibilities, which made them all the
more dangerous.

"We're not dealing with a simple shakedown,"
I said.

"I'll say one thing, Dinino would have been better off getting the money from a loan shark," Sam
said. "The vig to VISA is almost as bad as the vig
to some shylock on the street."

"I doubt that he didn't have the cash to send," I
said, "I think he *can't* send it. If Dinino is getting
blackmailed by these photos to the point that he
has to kidnap his own stepdaughter and threaten
to kill her so Gennaro will throw the race, then I'm
pretty sure his wife isn't aware of the situation.
He's setting Gennaro up so that whoever this third

party is will get a true windfall some other way,
not from him. This money is just to keep them
quiet until the race."

"You think he went to Bonaventura looking for
some quiet cash? I mean, what does fifty Gs mean
to Bonaventura, right?"

"Nothing," I said. "He spent more than that on
his daughter's birthday."

"He's already got protection," Sam said.

"Not the kind of protection Bonaventura could
offer," I said. "If he's getting pressed by some
other syndicate from back home, Bonaventura's a
big enough gun to maybe get them to back down.
Or force them to."

"Or short him some cash to get the problem
taken care of without alerting the missus," Sam
said. "It's not as if he can go to someone legit to
help him on this, because in ten minutes it would
be on some blog. Bonaventura is probably the only
person he knows who is in Miami who could help
him and not have it ping back to wifey."

"She finds out he's making time with a sixteen-
year-old girl, he loses everything," I said. "That's
the catalyst here." Which meant Fiona was right: It
all boiled down to a girl being involved. I just
wasn't expecting it to be an actual *girl*.

It also meant something a bit more distressing.

"If Dinino told Bonaventura even half of the
truth," I said, "if he really wanted to convince him
to help, then he told him about Maria and Liz on

the boat. Didn't tell him he was behind it, of course, but he must have dangled that out there."

"Oh, Mikey," Sam said. "That's not good."

"Yeah," I said. "That's occurring to me." My play this afternoon to get Bonaventura off Gennaro had probably worked. But now it's likely he thought Tommy the Ice Pick and his outfit were behind the blackmailing of Dinino, too. Or were at least affiliated with whoever was pulling the strings. It was, disturbingly, a perfect mess.

We knew Dinino was the one pressing Gennaro.

We knew why Dinino was pressing Gennaro, but not who was pressing Dinino.

We knew that if we released the photos to make Dinino fold, there was a good chance Maria and Liz would be dead and, in short order, Gennaro would be killed for ratting Bonaventura out, too.

"We need to get Maria and Liz off that boat," Sam said.

"Or we need to make sure that Bonaventura does it for us," I said.

Christopher Bonaventura's easiest move, provided he thought unemotionally, provided he had someone with a little tactical training in his stable, was to remove the chance Maria and Liz might get killed himself.

Which meant I needed to speak with my new friend Alex Kyle again sooner rather than later. Convince him that even if I wasn't Tommy the Ice Pick, I was still the person making this all happen.

"You know where Virgil is?" I asked.

"I'm sure I could find him," he said. "Spray a bit of your mother's perfume into the wind and he'll poke his head from his shell."

"Tell him we need a boat," I said, ignoring Sam.

"What are we looking at? Forty-footer? Cigar lounge with a stripper pole?"

"Something fast," I said. "It would be helpful if we didn't need to return it."

"I'll put out the word," he said.

Still, there was an unseen aspect to this all that was troubling me. Alex Kyle's admission that he knew me wasn't a move he *needed* to make.

Which meant it was a move he *had* to make.

The essence of developing warnings intelligence is the ability to understand that you can't concentrate solely on the evidence you have in front of you. You have to have the facility to look beyond what's happening now and decide what's going to happen next. A good spy makes reasoned predictions based on experience and then reacts accordingly.

This means occasionally you have to go into a small country and assassinate the president before anything outwardly untoward has happened.

It also means that occasionally you need to be aware that the gun is pointed at you.

Which was precisely what I was feeling when my cell rang. It was Fi.

"Where are you?" I asked.

"Meeting with Timothy Sherman's illegal driver," she said. "Or at least what's left of him."

"Fi," I said.

"He looks to have been a brainy individual."

"Tell me you didn't shoot him."

"I didn't shoot him."

"Good. Who did?"

"Judging from the spatter pattern, I'd say someone shooting from about a half mile away with a sniper rifle. Fascinating, really. I wish you were here to see it with me, Michael."

"Yeah," I said. Fi is one of those people who isn't fazed by violence and gore. It's the sort of thing she finds alluring, which is not the least of her mysteries. "I had my own spatter pattern today, so I'm good."

"Shame," she said.

"Fi, do you want to tell me where you are, or are you going to make me guess?"

"That's the funny thing, Michael," she said. "I'm standing on the sidewalk in front of your loft."

11

Fiona Glenanne has a unique worldview: it's her world and you would be wise not to get in the way. What this means in a practical sense is that she's pretty good at getting what she wants.

Shoes.

Purses.

The contents of a bank vault.

In the process of acquiring said items, she has no problem punching you in the throat, setting fire to your home or giving you the impression that you are mere moments away from a level of physical pleasure you've only read about in the Kama Sutra.

All of which makes her the perfect person to extract information from those who might be unwilling under normal circumstances to give it up.

Male.

Female.

It doesn't really matter.

So when she walked into the offices of the Star

Class Association looking for Timothy Sherman and encountered an armed female security guard at the front desk, she wasn't concerned in the least.

Women with guns were her comfort zone. Though, Fi couldn't abide the fact that she looked to be one of those women who clearly took part in weight-lifting competitions. It was the shock of white blond hair, the rub on tan that made her glow orange (and smell a bit like wet cardboard) and the forearms that looked like a freeway interchange with all the raised intersecting veins. Fiona thought that you could be dangerous without sacrificing style and grace and sex appeal. Never mind the horror of a rub on tan, just generally.

"Can I help you?" the guard asked. Her voice was a little on the thick side, too.

"Yes," Fi said. "I'm from Allied Car Rental and I'm afraid we have a very substantial problem. I need to see Mr. Sherman."

"Okay," she said. She looked down at the phone system, which struck Fiona as being a might too confusing for simple use. Didn't anyone have an intercom anymore? She guessed that people with impressive looking phone exchanges at their front desks wanted to give off the impression that they fielded many, many calls. Odd, really. Power through the impression of vast communication and heavily veined women with guns at the front desk.

The office itself was fairly standard: a rounded

off desk up front covered in trade magazines, including one, Fiona noted, that featured a photo of
Gennaro Stefania on the cover. He was cute, but
from what she'd learned, not much on the manly
side of things. Oh, he could pilot a boat, but she
doubted he could take a punch.

Men.

The shame of their sex was that so few lived up
to billing.

Beyond the desk was a locked glass door—
nothing special security-wise, Fiona saw, just a
keyed lock. Nothing exciting happened in these
offices, she imagined, and very little of value could
possibly be inside apart from computers and
phones and maybe a little petty cash. She could be
in and out of the place in five minutes with everything of worth and no one would probably raise
an eye, least of all the woman in front of her, who
was now punching buttons almost at random.

Fi saw that a rather pained look was beginning
to cast over the poor woman's face. Maybe she
was having some sort of anabolic issue.

"I'm not really the receptionist, so this phone is
like Swahili," the guard said. "I'm just here for
extra security and the receptionist is at lunch."

"Security?" Fi took a chance. "Because of that
explosion the other day?"

The guard smiled and Fi saw that her teeth
were insanely white. Nice teeth are important but
this was absurd. It was like she had a mouth filled

with piano keys. "Yes!" she said. "Omigod. Did
you hear about that? It's crazy, isn't it?"

"It is," Fi said. This security guard woman was
really quite the woman of multitudes. She pro-
jected strength and body dysmorphic issues, but
also seemed incredibly vapid. Very strange. "This
whole boating industry can be very dangerous."

The guard nodded her head, which was also a
strange exercise, since she nodded and blinked
excessively hard at the same time while keeping
the smile burnished on her face. "This is my only
day, but everyone at the agency was like, hey, you
might get to break an arm, Gretchen! And so I
thought, hey, when else do you get the chance to
break an arm in a really nice building like this
one? Mobsters and rappers and rich people. I
could really meet someone neat, right?"

Fi didn't really have a response to that. Chiefly
because none of it made any sense to her. She had
the impression that this was a woman used to
people not listening to her closely and thus no one
ever corrected her when she said absurd things. A
shame, really. A little molding and Fi thought she
could probably turn her into a fairly competent
knee-breaker. But she'd need to get rid of that tan
and that smile. It was all very off putting.

"Anywho," the guard said. She poked around
the phone some more. "I don't know how to get
Mr. Sherman on this thing. Do you know where
his office is at?"

"Yes," Fi said. She had a new opinion. Anyone who ended a sentence with the word "at" and managed to get the term "anywho" into a sentence was unmoldable at any cost. "If you'll just open the door, of course."

The security guard got up from behind the desk and made her way to the door to unlock it, which gave Fi a chance to look at the phone system and see that Mr. Sherman was in office 129. It was right on the phone in huge bold letters. It also said he was not to be disturbed until after the race. A very important man, no doubt, in the same way many people think they are very important: that their particular world is more interesting and important than yours.

That didn't jibe with Fi. Timothy Sherman, she thought, you're going to be picking flowers.

The interior offices of the Star Class Association resembled something put together by Gilligan and the Skipper: Nautical paintings on the walls, bits of ancient oars and masts and such encased in glass frames and boxes scattered down the long hallways. A cubicle farm painted light blue and with funny signs at their various nexuses that had arrows pointed to Bermuda, Cape Cod, Hawaii, the Tropic of Cancer. The cubicles themselves were largely empty, which made sense since all of the action was happening down in the marina in preparation for the race, but the few people she did see were all young men who looked like they'd been born wearing navy blue diapers.

Timothy Sherman's office was at the back of the floor and looked out over the cubicles in one direction and out towards the sea in the other. His door was open, presumably so the drones working away could periodically stand up and see out to the water and marvel at how lucky their boss was.

She already didn't like Timothy Sherman, which was nice since she hoped she'd get the chance to hurt him.

Just a little.

Maybe a pinch.

A tight squeeze.

A pistol whip to the eyebrow. Something worth the trouble she went to putting on the silly conservative suit she had to wear in order to look like a young car rental executive, never mind the tacky DayRunner she was using to hold documents.

When she reached Sherman's office door, she found him sitting with his back to the door, staring intently at his computer, which was filled with what looked to Fiona like weather reports and information on the tides. Very important stuff, no doubt.

"Timothy Sherman?" she said loudly, making him jump a bit in his seat. He turned and faced her and Fi saw that he was angry. He still had at least another few days before he could be disturbed, of course.

"Who are you?"

"Pitney Bowes from Allied Car Rental," she said and extended her hand for Sherman to shake, which he did. He was one of those guys who shook women's hands like he thought his strength might overpower them, so he intentionally went light, so Fi gave him all she had until he actually winced and pulled back. "Sir, we have a big problem."

She reached into the DayRunner and slid out a copy of the police report Loretta had made earlier involving a certain Peeping Tom. Fi had done a little work on the report, adding the plate of the rental to it, and Sherman's name, too.

Sherman read the report silently, apart from the growing sound of his labored breathing, and then set it down.

"This is a big misunderstanding," he said.

"Mr. Sherman, you understand that it's bad public relations when our cars are used in the commission of a sex crime, don't you?"

"Of course," he said. "But that wasn't what was happening. I wasn't even there. I've been right here all day."

"So the car drove itself?"

"No, no," he said. "I'm afraid the car was in use for official Cup business, but I certainly wasn't the driver and I can assure you that the person driving the car was not engaged in any crime."

It was really too bad Sherman wasn't the ultimate criminal here, Fi thought, because there was just something about him that annoyed her. It was probably that he used the term "official Cup business" as if it meant something she should be impressed with.

"Mr. Sherman, there are no other drivers listed on your rental contract," Fi said. "I'm going to have to contact your insurance agency and, I'm not afraid to say, you are civilly liable if poor Ms. Loretta, who I must say sounded terribly distraught, chooses to litigate."

Ah, the word that makes men of a certain ilk quake: litigate.

"We don't need to go in that direction, do we?" Sherman said. He was smiling now, confident, like he'd been in this position before. He reached into his desk and pulled out an envelope, flipped through the contents and then came out with a ticket. "I would love for you to be my special guest on our hospitality yacht to watch the first half of the Cup."

"That's very generous," Fi said and returned Sherman's smile, even gave an extra flourish with her eyes, licked her lips twice, let him really think that a ticket on a yacht was just the sort of thing a girl like her would really want. She kept that look of honest rapture and joy on her face as she said, "But I still need the driver's name, or else I'm afraid the police will be showing up here in about an hour to arrest you, and so I can stop my assistant from calling your insurance carrier to let them know of the malfeasance your organization has been party to."

Sherman swallowed hard. "His name is Robert Roberge."

Not a name he wanted to give up. Interesting, Fi thought. Now that he was frightened, she had him precisely where she wanted him. Scared people think they can talk their way out of problems, think that by giving up the information you ask for that they'll stay out of trouble, particularly someone like Sherman, who seemed like he had something to hide, or at least something he didn't want to tell the kind woman from Allied Car Rental.

"Social security number?" Fiona said, thinking, what the hell, why not fish a bit. Besides, she needed to get him out of the office for a few moments so she could plant a wire in the room, since she figured the real interesting news would come after she left.

"Why do you need that?"

"Mr. Sherman, do you see this?" She waved the police report. "This is not a joke, sir. This is the police."

"I'll need to get his file," he said. He was positively bashful as he walked out of his office, perhaps because he saw his entire career flashing before his eyes. Wait until he found out his race was fixed.

Fiona would have felt slightly sorry for him if he'd been gentleman enough to offer her two tickets for the yacht party; one ticket was just smarmy. And anyway, she didn't have time to feel much of anything. She needed to get Sherman's office rigged for sound.

It used to be that getting a surreptitious wire on someone took tremendous sleight of hand and incredible risk.

That was before cell phones.

Cell phones have two notable characteristics that make them excellent for use in clandestine operations in suburban settings: They are easily lost and entirely nonthreatening. So if you want to wire someone who wouldn't normally be looking for such things, all you need are two cell phones, one to leave sitting open in the vicinity of the person you're interested in and one pressed to your ear listening in.

A fully charged cell phone battery will last three days, which should be more than enough time to glean the information you desire.

Fiona opted for the fake tree sitting on top of the file cabinet just adjacent to Sherman's desk. She noted the faux leaves were dusty, which meant it had probably been a good week, probably more, since the cleaning crew in the building had bothered to run a feather duster over the atrocity. Fiona thought that having a fake plant in Miami was a sin just as egregious as the fake tan out front. Some things just didn't need to be replicated when the original was perfectly well and good.

A few moments later, Sherman returned holding Roberge's file. It wasn't terribly thick, though Fiona thought there was probably something of interest to be gleaned from having a look inside.

"His number is 534-24 . . ." Sherman started.

"435, okay," Fiona said. "What was next?"

"No," Sherman said, "534."

"534," she said, writing while she spoke, "25, you said?"

"No," Sherman said. He repeated it again and Fiona pretended to take it down, and then read it back to Sherman, all in the wrong order again, which seemed to frustrate poor Mr. Sherman.

When she couldn't get the spelling of Roberge's name down—nor his driver's license, or his address, all information needed for the application, and so she could have one of Sam's buddies run a background on him, provided she didn't get everything she wanted just by asking Mr. Sherman—it appeared to Fi that Sherman was about to have a stroke.

Fiona could smell perspiration and not the healthy, clean kind, but the kind that is generated when your body goes into fight-or-flight mode. "Here," he said, and tossed the file to Fiona. "It's all right there on the front page. Just copy it yourself. Okay? Just copy it yourself!"

He sat back in his chair and laced his fingers on

top of his head, gathered up his hair and tugged. Not a good day to be king.

Roberge's employment file noted that he worked as security guard for the company. It also noted that he'd previously been convicted of a felony. On the line where it said, "If Yes, Please Explain" Roberge had scrawled, all in caps AS-SAULT, EXTORTION, ETC. It shuddered Fiona to imagine what ETC. meant. If you put assault and extortion on an application, what aren't you admitting? Drowning puppies?

She handed the file back to Sherman, who looked at it like it was contagious. "Job title?" Fiona said, even though she already knew. Didn't want poor Mr. Sherman to know she'd been peeking, though it's hardly covert activity when you do it right in front of someone; though it must have been hard for Mr. Sherman to pay attention to much of anything at that moment.

"Consultant," Sherman said. "Security."

Companies who hired ex-cons for security deserved all of the bad things that happened to them. Personally, Fiona thought she had a very strong work ethic and while she occasionally worked on the other side of the law, it wasn't like she was breaking arms for drugs. Robbing a bank is a victimless crime, really. And selling guns, well, at least in America people had the right to bear arms. She was sure most people who purchased guns from her did so for perfectly reasonable purposes. And anyway, it wasn't her commitment in question. If people needed guns, they'd get them from somewhere.

"And purpose of Mr. Roberge's presence at the location?" Again, Sherman looked nervous, maybe on the verge of tears. "Sir, it's required for the insurance. If we do this the right way, your insurance won't be contacted, the police won't press charges and everyone sleeps like little babies."

"He was investigating a possible security breach," Sherman said. "Look, Ms. Bowes? I can't have this getting in the newspaper, okay? This is really sensitive. The slightest sense of impropriety and this whole race could go down the tubes. Did you see that yacht that blew up? Those are the kinds of people who want to breach security, ma'am. Mr. Roberge was sent to check out a possible negative, uh, person of interest. That's all I can say."

A negative person of interest. That's all he *had* to say.

"All right," Fiona said. She figured her ruse could only last so long and that if she kept hammering Sherman, he might not last much more, either. "All I need is Mr. Roberge's signature on this form and I think we can avoid prosecution."

"He's not here," Sherman said.

Of course he wasn't. Fi suspected he was lurking about the city somewhere, however. And it would be good to know where that was. "Well, if you can fax the form back to our office by five this evening, I think that should be fine."

"Yes, yes, fine," he said. He stood up and Fiona decided to give the man his dignity and allow him to dictate when the meeting was over. Besides, she was eager to get to her car to hear his next conversation.

She walked back through the cubicle maze and into the foyer, where unfortunately the receptionist was back on duty and the security guard woman was now standing and looking threatening by the door, though when Fiona got near she gave her a nice smile. "Everything go well?" she asked Fi.

"Crisis averted," she said. The guard looked saddened by this. "But I'm sure something bad will happen later."

Unfortunately for the security guard, it turned out the bad thing wasn't going to happen on her watch. This was made clear to Fi as she slipped her cell phone from her purse and listened in on Timothy Sherman's conversation. He was screaming obscenities at someone, telling them they'd nearly destroyed the entire boating organization with their stupidity and that if he didn't get a signature from him there was a good chance someone from "Catch A Predator" would be waiting for him at his shitty apartment when he got off work. He then told the man—presumably Roberge—to stay right where he was, that he was bringing the form to him.

Fi got into her car and waited for Sherman to appear, which he did a few moments later. He jumped into a matching Lexus—this one had the official seal of the race stuck to the side door, like he was a real estate agent—and pulled out of the lot.

Fi didn't think she needed to be particularly savvy in her tail, since it was clear Sherman wasn't looking to be followed, particularly since he was talking into a cell phone the entire time he drove and nearly sideswiped a bus and then quite nearly rammed a Miata being driven by a woman who literally had blue hair.

While paying attention to surroundings was not Sherman's strong suit, it was Fiona's, and when it became clear after twenty minutes of driving that she was following Sherman back to a rather familiar destination—a loft above a nightclub in a not so nice part of town—she began to realize things we're not going to be as simple as planned. So when Sherman made his final turn down the street where the loft is, Fi just kept going, especially since she could hear an ambulance siren in the distance and saw that people were mingling on the sidewalk and looking about with their hands over their mouths. Never a good sign.

Fi parked her car around the other side of the block and walked to the mouth of the street, where another group of people were already assembling.

There was a fire engine, a Lexus and quite a bit of mess on the street. And Timothy Sherman walking towards the scene in what looked to be a rather significant state of agitation. "What happened?" Fi said to a teenage boy wearing a backwards Marlins cap.

"Man got shot," he said. He pointed to the Lexus. "Half his head is over there on the ground." He was so nonchalant it almost startled Fi. She looked at where the kid was pointing and sure enough, a good portion of Roberge's head was on the pavement, along with glass and blood and brain matter. Bad day to be Rob Roberge, Fi thought. After spending some time observing the scene, she decided it would be prudent to give me a call and fill me in.

"Still not seeing the funny," I said when she was through.

"Neither was Mr. Sherman's proxy," she said.

"He look to be involved?" I said.

"He seems to be cooperating with the police, mostly by sobbing and shaking."

"Who would have wanted us away from Gennaro?" I said, but even as I said it, I knew the answer. The only way someone would know about me as it related to Gennaro prior to my meeting with Bonaventura this morning would be if they were privy to our conversation at the Setai the night previous. Which meant Dinino. But it didn't explain why this poor sap was dead on my street.

"I think you've been set up, Michael," she said. "I think you've been given a nice round of diversions."

"Seems that way," I said.

"Who do I get to shoot?"

"I'll let you know," I said. "Stay close and I'll call you when I know what the plan is."

"Yay," she said without much enthusiasm.

I hung up with Fi and looked back outside. Gennaro was still making adjustments on his boat. He was due to launch shortly.

"You need to stay here and watch Gennaro while he's on land and on the water. He's not safe."

"What do you mean?"

"I mean there's a good chance someone might shoot him."

"What's going on?"

"Timothy Sherman's driver from yesterday is dead," I said. "And I have a pretty good feeling that Dinino bugged Gennaro's room at the Setai. We're in the middle of something here, Sam, and it's not just about this job."

"Got it, Mikey." He dusted off the rest of his beer and stood up. "Sea looks nice and calm."

"That's the bay. The sea is a little farther out."

Sam seemed to consider this. "You think they sell Dramamine in this joint somewhere?"

"Maybe try the gift shop," I said. "Maybe see if they have more appropriate clothes, too. When you get back, get your friend Jimenez on the phone and have him find out who planted this girl, who might have the juice to pull something like this on Dinino. I need a name."

"Mikey, it's nine hours ahead of us in Italy right now. It's the middle of the night."

"Your friend Jimenez got us into this," I said. "He can have a sleepless night."

Sam agreed, if begrudgingly. "Where you gonna be?"

"I need to have a conversation with Alex Kyle," I said.

"You're not going back to Bonaventura's, are you?"

"No," I said. "I'm pretty sure Alex Kyle will find me."

"This boat you want," Sam said, "can Virgil be on it?"

I liked Virgil.

Really.

It was just that Virgil meant my mother, and my mother meant problems.

"If he has to be," I said.

"The man is a valuable asset," Sam said.

"Make it happen," I said, "however it happens."

When Sam left, I called Nate and told him that I needed another favor.

"You need me or Slade Switchblade?"

"Slade Switchblade?"

"If you're Tommy the Ice Pick," he said, "I'm Slade Switchblade."

"When was the last time you actually *saw* a switchblade, Nate?"

"When was the last time you actually *saw* an ice pick, Michael?" Nate said. I paused. The truth was that the last time I saw an ice pick, I was shoving it into a man's chest in Siberia, so, best as I could recall, about the fall of 1999. But my hesitation was enough of an opening for Nate. "And anyway, it's about reputation, right? Isn't that what you said? So maybe Slade used a switchblade back in the day, and now, now he uses a howitzer, but no one knows. People are more scared of a switchblade than a howitzer, right? More personal, right? So that's why he's Slade Switchblade not Slade Howitzer."

"Right," I said. While I liked that Nate had actually thought through his own personal narrative, I wasn't comfortable with it actually making sense. "Look, I don't need Slade. But if I do, you give him whatever nickname you want."

"Slade Six-Gun was another one I came up with," he said.

"Great," I said. "If Wyatt Earp comes through town, I'll let him know you're ready to mount up. In the meantime, I need you to talk to your friends in the betting industries. Find out who is putting money against the *Pax Bellicosa* in the Miami-to-Nassua. Not five hundred or even a thousand dollars, but numbers with lots of zeros."

"Someone rich rolling," he said.

"Uh, yeah," I said. "Someone rich rolling. Anyone owes you any favors, I need you to call them in." Nate was silent. I thought I heard him writing something down. "You still there?"

"Just getting this all on paper so I don't forget anything."

I've never, ever, seen Nate take a note, or make note, mentally, of anything. "Okay," I said. "You run into a problem, let me know."

"I got nintey-nine problems," Nate said, "but this ain't one of 'em." When I didn't respond, he said, "It's a song, Michael. One day, when you're free, we should sit down and I'll catch you up on the parts of the twenty-first century you've missed out on."

"I'd like that," I said.

After I hung up with Nate, I watched Gennaro from the window of the Aground until I finally saw Sam striding through the marina. He had on a striped shirt, blue pants, a white baseball cap and bright red boat shoes, all of which made him look like a waiter at a nautical-theme restaurant at Disney World. He'd have to tell Gennaro's crew some plausible story, but I wasn't too worried. I had a good feeling that expert sailor Chuck Finley was about to be on the deck.

12

Anxiety—like its cousin, actual physical pain—is a natural occurrence. It's your brain's way of reminding you that even if your ancestors didn't see a saber-toothed tiger lurking in the low underbrush, there was a high probability that the tiger was there, licking its chops, anticipating the rich and nuanced flavors found in your average australopithecine.

Where you might find a therapist to talk you through your anxiety, maybe find a way to medicate the fear of the tiger away, when you're a spy, you learn to calculate your anxiety so that you can compartmentalize it in your mind and make decisions, so that if a house cat crosses your path you don't scramble an F-16 from an offshore aircraft carrier to take it out.

What are you afraid of?

Is the threat credible?

Can you take it out by yourself?

Unbounded anxiety creates mental isolation.

Even a spy can go crazy if he's not able to exercise his brain. If you're captured by the enemy, hooded and shoved into a locked room, the first thing you should do is start talking to yourself. Even if you're speaking gibberish, you want to use the only weapon you have—your intellect—to turn your fear into your asset. Language and thought and reason will focus you, will break down your anxiety into workable parts, until you see your anxiety for what it ultimately is: a desire not to die or suffer terrible pain. Once you recognize the danger and the possible outcomes, it's easier to fight, even if the fight is all in your head.

If someone really wanted you dead, you'd already be dead.

While I didn't know precisely what I was facing, I knew that the players on my radar were not much to be afraid of personally, but for Gennaro and his wife and child, however, they were the epitome.

I had to remember that.

I was also aware that positions were aligning in such a way that even if I was able to save Gennaro's family, I might very well be in the crosshairs of the bad guys, the good guys and probably a few opportunists, too.

That meant the threat was credible.

And that meant I needed help.

The sun was already down, but Bayfront Park,

Miami's own central park, was lit with glittering white bulbs strung tree to tree to highlight a free show given by the Flying Trapeze School housed on the park's grounds. There were booths selling corn dogs, pork sandwiches, funnel cakes and sweet corn on the cob, others offering hand-churned ice cream, fried plantains and guava marmalade served over pound cake. Young couples and families sat on blankets and watched the spectacle as the trapeze students sailed through the air, catching each other by the ankles and flying back again, flipping, twirling, and even falling occasionally to the mesh net below, to the *ooohs* and *ahhhs* of the crowd. There was that whirl of expectation in the air that comes from shared excitement and fear.

The festive kind of fear.

Somewhere, Fiona was watching my back. If real trouble came down, she'd be on top of it. That allowed me to focus my attention on the task at hand, which was locating Barry, Miami's finest nonviolent lowlife, among the audience of sugar-high kids and their parents.

I eventually found him sitting on a lawn chair under a tree, a plate of food on his lap, a cooler beside him.

Barry was the kind of guy who could get you what you needed, like dummy home loans, millions of dollar in fake wire transfers, new identities, small helicopters, and the occasional piece of advice about the inner workings of the bad people he associated with.

A jack-of–all-criminal-trades, really.

I sat down on the grass next to him, and for a few minutes we watched the trapeze. Four different students were doing a series of tricks that involved midair flips timed perfectly to a classical music arrangement. There was always someone in the air and someone launching into the air.

The precision, timing and dedication looked flawless, but it meant hours of preparation and failure had been embarked on long before this date.

"What I wonder," Barry said after a while, "is what a professional trapeze artist does on his day off. Sit in a cubicle?"

"Probably the same thing anyone does," I said.

"What do you do?"

"I plot," I said. "And wait."

"See, that's the thing," Barry said. "You need to find something more relaxing. I tried collecting wine for a little while. You know, like as a hobby? Started going to tastings and these things where they put out ten different kinds of cheeses and then the wine you're supposed to drink with each cheese. Turned out to be very stressful. Too many decisions to make."

"What do you do now?"

"I started getting into chakra cleansing," he

said. "Girl I was dating was a big advocate, but that didn't do the trick, either. She was very spiritual about it, always telling me to surrender to the release, but I just couldn't get into that. I feel like my chakra is pretty healthy."

"That's what you're known for," I said. "That and bad checks."

"This was supposed to be my day off," Barry said. "And here I am, sitting next to Mr. Marked for Death."

"Think how I feel," I said.

Barry hadn't actually looked at me yet. Or if he had, I couldn't tell since he was still wearing his sunglasses. Maybe he was waiting for a break in the action.

"Have to say," he said, "I was little surprised to hear from you. Today of all days."

"Yeah?"

"Word is you got a bullet to the dome this afternoon, actually."

"That was someone else," I said.

"What happened to your forehead?"

"Christopher Bonaventura punched it," I said.

"You wake up in the morning and this stuff just happens, or is there an order to it?"

"Depends what morning it is," I said.

"Maybe you just live in a bad neighborhood."

"No," I said, "the guy who was shot in front of my place was probably taken out by a sniper, so they could have been in another neighborhood completely. I suppose they could have been in a high-rise a half a mile away." I pointed at the towering buildings across the street from the park. "Like one of those."

"Comforting," Barry said.

"Any other words being thrown out about me?"

"Only that since you got back into town, the number of professional killers enjoying the sun and beaches has increased tenfold. I'm thinking of starting a side business selling maps to your place."

"Yeah," I said, "about that. You got anything on an ex-Marine named Alex Kyle doing business out here?"

"Big guy?"

"Big enough."

"Rolls with ten guys who look just like him?"

"Yeah," I said.

Barry pulled off his sunglasses and rubbed them on his shirt. Held them up. Looked through them. Put 'em right back on. "Lot of fake passports in town this week," Barry said, like I hadn't asked him about Alex Kyle. "Lots of people asking for private protection. Big money getting tossed around. Heard there was a guy trying to move yellow cake who was staying at a condo, taking meetings on his deck, like it was nothing. Another guy supposedly was trying to move weapons-grade plutonium. FBI picked him up eating sushi next to Bono."

One of the trapeze artists failed to catch his partner, and the partner—a young Asian woman who looked to weigh less than a hundred pounds—sailed into the netting below, eliciting a collective moan from the crowd. She popped back up quickly, but looked dazed and somewhat unbalanced.

"You think that hurts?" Barry said.

"Any time you fall from the sky onto the ground," I said, "it hurts."

"You ever jump out of a plane?"

"A few times," I said.

"That seems relaxing," he said.

"Not if the people on the ground are shooting at you," I said.

"Can't control that," Barry said. He reached into his cooler and pulled out a bottle of beer and handed it to me, took another one out for himself. He looked at me then and clanked his bottle into mine in a toast. "To life, then," he said, and then drank from his bottle slowly, like he was thinking about something particularly vexing.

"Something on your mind, Barry?"

"This Alex Kyle," Barry said, "he's not a nice person."

I thought about it. "No. Probably not."

"Wasn't really a question," Barry said. "Just an observation." He broke off a piece of fried plantain from his plate and chewed on it carefully. "Anyway," he said, "now that you're alive again, I'm just saying you should look into ways to spend your free time that are less hazardous to your health. You never hear about anyone getting gunned down while building model planes in their garage."

He had a point, though if I took to building model planes in my garage, I might be inclined to gun myself down.

"I need a favor," I said.

"Last favor I did for you? The IRS audited my nana *the next day*. That's not right."

"Nana good with keeping receipts?"

"She's been dead for fifteen years," Barry said.

"Tell me you're not cashing your grandmother's social security checks," I said.

"You watch the news? It's important to tighten up where you can. Besides, it helps to have an extra social security number or two for a rainy day, like if some ex-spy puts your business in peril and you need to relocate and start all over."

"You help me here," I said, "I'll owe you."

"You already owe me," he said.

I looked around. "Dinner with Fiona," I said. I paused. Waited for a sign. Like a shank to the neck. When none came, I continued with "My treat."

"She's not a nice person, either," Barry said.

"No," I said, "she's not."

"That's kind of hot, isn't it?"

"It is."

Barry chewed on another bit of plantain. "This one of those 'or people will die' things?"

"Yeah," I said. I showed him the paperwork on the credit transfer to Myanmar. "You ever do any business with this bank?"

Barry visibly recoiled in his chair, enough so that he had to grab his plate before it tipped off his lap. "Myanmar is off-limits," he said.

"How can an entire country be off-limits?" I said.

"I don't know," he said, "maybe I'm just averse to having the government disappear me. Or being called a terrorist and shipped to some torture chamber on a boat. Or having everyone I know murdered in the night by people like yourself. No offense."

"None taken," I said.

"Or your friend Mr. Kyle."

"Have you talked to him, Barry?"

"He paid me a visit."

"What was he looking for?"

"You," he said.

"What did you tell him?"

"The truth," Barry said. "That the last time we did business my nana got audited. Told him I was out of the Michael Westen business until Nana's IRS problems disappeared."

"I appreciate that," I said.

"Consider it the advantage of working with local businesses," he said.

"I still need a favor," I said.

"I still get dinner with Fiona?"

Even though I couldn't see Fi, her presence, at least mentally, was weighing on me. I tweaked the offer accordingly. "I can guarantee that you will eat in the same room with her," I said. "Everything else is up to chance."

"All a man can ask," he said.

"How much time would you need to get a hold of a couple hundred credit card numbers?"

"How much are you willing to pay?"

"Whatever it takes to get your nana's legal issues resolved," I said. "And I'll pay double if you can get them from Russia, Japan, Saudi Arabia— any place with a lot of banks and a lot of regulations."

"How long would you need them for?"

"About ten minutes," I said.

"I wasn't planning on working tonight," Barry said. "But I guess I could make a couple calls."

I handed him the bank information again, and this time he took it. "I want you to flood this account with transactions," I said. "Charges. Cash advances. It doesn't matter. But max every single card. I want an international banking incident."

Barry shook his head. "You got maybe fifteen minutes before the banks on both ends freeze all the transactions," Barry said. "That bank in Myanmar? It doesn't matter if it's run by Al Qaeda or the CIA, the computers will still autolock the account, thinking it's being cracked. You'll never see a single cent."

"That's the idea," I said. If my hunch was correct, whoever operated the bank account Dinino was transferring money into would be expecting far more money after Gennaro lost. Bonaventura probably wasn't the only one taking action. But that would be difficult to achieve if their bank account was being investigated by every major credit fraud agency in the world. And if the U.S. government and its allies were monitoring it for money going to terrorists, it would take about thirty seconds for that account to get flagged by the kinds of people who you do not want flagging your accounts. The kinds of people who don't mind coming across enemy lines to make sure you understand that your banking interests are very, very interesting indeed. By flooding it ten minutes before the race, it ensured me a window of time to confirm Maria and Liz were safe. Once the people who operated it found out Dinino wasn't going to be able to make due, there was going to be . . . issues.

"I need to worry about anyone coming after me?"

"Anyone comes near you," I said, "they're coming through me first."

"Really?"

"Really. What are friends for?"

"Is that what we are?"

I had to think about it. "I guess so," I said.

"Nice to know. And not that I don't trust you,

but soon as they start bouncing back the charges,"
Barry said, "Barry bounces out of Miami."

"I'd recommend that," I said. "I'll call you when
I want you to start and then lose your phone."

"And then, what, Fiona catches up to me?"

"Uh, yeah," I said. "She'll be in contact."

We sat for a few moments longer and watched
the trapeze show. The Asian girl who'd fallen earlier was back on the swing now and picking up
momentum to perform another trick, her eyes
wide open, her face perfectly still, as if she'd completely forgotten that only a few minutes before
she fell to earth with a thud.

You spend the majority of your life in the company of spies and you begin to realize certain
truths, chief among them that in order to be a
good spy, you have to love your job.

Statistically speaking, this is unusual.

Most people hate their jobs.

Most people wish they were doing something
more interesting with their lives. So they go home
and they watch television shows about people
they can never be, or they read books about fan-
tasy worlds they'll never inhabit, or they get on to
the Internet and take on a persona, either on a
message board or in a role-playing game, and they
while away their free time pretending and then
wake up the next day and head back to the cubicle
maze.

But when you're a spy, every day has the potential to be completely unlike the previous day.

That kind of adrenaline is difficult to replace.

I wanted to solve my burn notice and get my job back not merely because I wasn't overly fond of being manipulated by forces that wanted to use me for their own devices, nor because I found their belief that I'd capitulate to their will—as however many other burned agents had over the years—specifically rude and disrespectful, never mind that it's never fun being shot at on a regular basis.

No, I wanted to solve my burn notice because I wanted my life back—the life I'd chosen.

Dealing with the mundane was not a job I was uniquely qualified for, nor, I suspected, was it made for Alex Kyle.

Which is why I wasn't surprised to see him sitting on the hood of my Charger. That Fiona was sitting next to him, eating a Popsicle, was not in the game plan.

They made a rather striking couple, actually.

I'd parked the car in the lot across from the park, the most public spot, so the two of them were sitting beneath the glow of a towering streetlight and right next to the cashier's kiosk.

I reached under the back of my shirt, where my gun was stashed against my back, and clicked off the safety, anyway. My loft might not be in the most public locale, but there is a nightclub beneath it, which makes it sort of an odd place to assassinate someone, but no less odd than a brightly lit parking lot swarming with people.

Better safe than dead.

"So you two have met," I said. "That's nice."

"Alex was just telling me about your performance this afternoon."

"Vintage work," Alex said.

"Thank you," I said. "Fiona? A word?" Fiona slid off the hood of the Charger and I took her by the arm and guided her a few steps away.

I smiled.

It was the only way I could keep from screaming.

"Care to explain?"

"He was trying to break into your car to leave you a message," she said. "I offered to sit with him instead and we'd wait for you together."

"That makes *perfect* sense," I said.

"He's off the clock, Michael."

"A guy like him is never off the clock," I said.

"Anyway," Fiona said, "I explained to him that we didn't appreciate his meddling in our business with Gennaro. It's not his place, professionally, to get between you and your ability to make a living. I think he respected my honesty. Of course, I had a gun pointed at his midsection at the time." She licked her Popsicle. "But he was even kind enough to purchase me this lovely frozen treat afterward. He's been very polite."

"I'm happy to hear you've bonded," I said.

"He's very friendly."

"He threatened to kill Nate today," I said.

Fiona considered this. "No one is the ideal," she said. "And anyway, I made him put all of his guns in your trunk. He's an unarmed man now."

"How did you manage that?" I said and dangled my keys in front of her.

"I have my own set now," she said.

"Since when?"

"You have your secrets," she said, "I have mine."

We stepped back over to the car, and Fi sat back down on the hood next to Alex.

"Where's Spock?" Alex said.

"Pardon me?"

"Well," he said, "you're the Captain Kirk here, right? And my new friend must be Bones. Where is Spock? Big guy? Drinks a lot? Lost his dog this morning? Because I can only assume that your brother—Slade, is that right?—is not the center of logic in your operation. More like one of those guys in red who beams down and dies first."

"You'd be surprised," I said.

Alex shrugged. "Maybe. Maybe. I'm surprised you're in the extortion business now, so there's that."

"You do what you have to do," I said. "We all have to eat. Luckily, I happen to like what I do, just like you."

"You like to kill women and children now, too?"

"That's my job," Fiona said. "Michael doesn't have the stomach for it."

Alex took that in. "Oh, I doubt that," he said after a time. "There are children in some developing nations who run screaming when they see a pair of sunglasses and a nice smile."

"What are we doing here?" I said.

"Three adults having a conversation," Alex said.

"Your boss know you're here?"

"He's not my boss," Alex said. "Just a consulting job. Something to pass the time. Keep my friends employed. Like I said. I found myself in Miami and needed some work."

"You just found yourself here?"

"Well, no," he said. "I came here to kill you. Brought my whole team."

Fiona nodded at me. "See, Michael, I told you he was polite."

"Who sent you?" I said.

"Who didn't? There are open contracts on you all across the world. I figured I'd claim them all."

"And yet here I am."

"We could have taken you out a dozen times," he said. "You don't exactly put yourself in the best company. Cut-rate arms dealers. Bank robbers. Forgers. Russians. That whack job Larry. Not exactly the Dirty Dozen."

"You know Larry?" I said.

"I did some work with him in Kosovo," Alex said.

"Was this before or after he was dead?"

"After," he said. "But he's one who's done it right. Sticks by his principles. Makes a good living. You, you're not even using your skills anymore. Just a petty crook half the time. And this business with the Ottones. The Michael Westen I heard about all these years would have put Dinino down for what he's doing with that girl, wouldn't have even bothered to extort from him. It's disgraceful, if you want my opinion, but like you said, we all have to eat."

There was a part of me that wanted to pull out my gun and shoot Alex Kyle between the eyes. It was a part of me that I didn't particularly like, a part of me that I'd kept pretty well in check since getting back to Miami.

"That's me," I said. "Big disgrace."

We stared at each other for a moment, and I could feel him making decisions, figuring out maybe his information was wrong. "Anyway," he said, "whoever wants you alive has more power than the people who want you dead. And has better technology. Five times in the last year I thought we had you. Five times I had to claim a corpse."

"It took you five dead bodies to figure this out?"

Alex shrugged again. "You're still Michael

Westen. I just figured you were hard to kill. I didn't realize you had guardian angels."

I looked at Alex sitting there on my Charger. I thought about all the men he'd sent to kill me who had died. Thought about the reasons behind it—pure, unadulterated greed—and felt something surge inside of me.

"Here I am," I said. "Only person to stop you is Fiona. And you could take her out, I'm sure."

Alex gave a slight chuckle. "Last guy I sent? Former Army Ranger. Kills on every continent. Damn near had ESP. Whoever is watching you left a note, carved into his back like scrimshaw, letting me know that they were aware of the situation and monitoring it closely and that if anyone was going to kill you, it was going to be them. So you'll pardon me for not taking you up on your kind offer."

"Then what are you doing here?" I said.

Alex got off my car and stretched his back, cracked his neck, ran through each knuckle on both of his hands.

"Professional courtesy," he said. "Mr. Bonaventura decides he wants you dead, there's nothing I can do about that. You came to him, I didn't come to you, so the rules are different here. Strictly business, Michael, but not spy business. I want that known."

"Right," I said. "You'll light me the fuck up, as I recall. You're just not going to be the one to pull the trigger, are you?"

"I'm just a consultant. He kills you, it's not like I end up any richer. And I don't claim it. I don't endorse it. But I will say that you don't go in and threaten someone like Mr. Bonaventura and not expect recrimination. And while I don't approve of what you're doing to Mr. Dinino or Mr. Stefania, that's your business."

I could hear some hesitation in Alex's voice. Gone was the brazen Jarhead of this afternoon and gone, too, was the confident version I found sitting next to Fiona mere minutes previous.

He was pleading for his life.

"Did you endorse killing the guy in front of my house today?"

"That wasn't me," he said.

"No?"

"If someone is dead near you, it's them or it's because of them. That's what I'm telling you."

Them.

"No," Fiona said, "what you're telling us is that you're scared and don't want to die. So I suggest you scurry back to your hole."

Alex Kyle looked around himself, figuring, I'm sure, that there was a gun trained on him somewhere. Maybe there was. Maybe there was one on all of us. "Not a lot of places to hide on the open sea between here and Nassau," he said. "You want to make sure you live another day, I'd leave Maria and Liz Ottone alone. You want to press Nicholas Dinino? Fine. Have at him. Scumbag, in my opinion. But you drag Mr. Bonaventura into this, you drag everyone you've met into it. And that's forever with him."

"I feel pretty protected," I said. "Five for five, right?"

"It won't always be like that," he said.

"And if that's the case," I said, "you can bet that I'll come looking for you first. And Alex? Ask those kids about the smile and the sunglasses, they'll tell you some stories."

"I'll do that," he said. He checked his watch. "Boy, it's late. And I think we've both got a long day tomorrow. I don't suppose you want to give me back my guns?"

"Good guess," I said.

A smirk ran across Alex Kyle's face. "Tommy the Ice Pick. The funny thing? You check out. You got wise guys who swear to your veracity. Bonaventura actually believes someone called Tommy the Ice Pick has him cornered on a potential murder rap." He shook his head once, very slowly, and started backing away from us. A black SUV pulled into the parking lot right on cue and idled next to him. "He killed his own father and brother and didn't get caught, and you actually have him worried." He patted the hood of the SUV. "All else fails, you got that going for you."

Alex Kyle got into the SUV then and pulled away, even offered a brusque wave out the window as he passed us.

"He was nice," Fi said. "And he donated some very nice guns to our rebel cause."

"That's good," I said. "But I don't think we'll need them."

"Don't be such a *disgrace*," Fiona said. "We could have been killing people and improving your standing among your peers all the while. We should take up that opportunity now that we have it."

"Next time," I said. We got in the Charger and headed back toward Fiona's.

My cell rang. It was Nate. I answered in one ring. Never too late to set a good example.

"You owe me big, bro," Nate said.

"What do you have?"

"You ever hear of a country called Calabria?"

"It's not a country," I said. "It's a province. In Italy. On the Ionian Sea." I remembered I was talking to Nate and added, "It's the part that looks like the toe of the boot."

"Awesome," Nate said. "We ever get on a game show together, you'll handle world geography questions and I'll be the guy saving lives."

Nate with confidence was a scary thing. It presupposed a level of involvement in my affairs that usually promised bad things.

But maybe this time was different.

The idea of a game show involving geography and death did, admittedly, have some allure.

"Slade Switchblade came in handy tonight,"

Nate said. "I called in all the favors I had—and that reminds me, next week, no rush, but a friend of mine is going to need some help with an ex-girlfriend who is stalking him. I waived your normal fee, but said you'd take care of whatever problems existed in an expedient and spyish fashion that would be totally badass to witness. He wants her car to blow up, but I said, 'Hey, no promises.'"

"Nate," I said. "Get to it."

"Right, right." He explained that a friend of his was picking up some "businessmen" at the airport and bringing them to a race party at South Beach and that in the past, he'd gotten the impression they were in the Mafia. "The real Mafia," Nate clarified. "So I tell him, 'Hey, this isn't something to trifle with; let me and my big bro take care of it.'"

"Tell me you didn't threaten these guys," I said. The last thing I needed on my plate now was even more angry crime bosses, which reminded me I was still angry with Sam for getting me in their business again. Next job he offered I was going to demand that he first provide expert witness testimony that whatever bad guys we were about to engage had more petty concerns than perpetuating a myth of toughness and respect based on a bullshit code from the last century.

"I'm not stupid," Nate said. "I just recorded them. But here's the thing. One guy wasn't even

Italian. He was Iranian. Or Iraqi. One of those places where they don't use the alphabet."

When you're xenophobic, not knowing the difference between Iranian, Iraqi or any other Middle Eastern point of origin makes you dangerous. When you're a common person who can't pinpoint the 50 states on a map, much less imagine explaining Puerto Rico's role, it just makes you ignorant, but not uncommon. In Nate's case, this was the latter. What was notable about Calabria was not that it was in Italy, but that it's also home to traditionally the largest concentration of Muslims in the country—in Italy, over one-third of the country is Muslim—and normally that only means good things.

In Calabria, however, the international crime trade and terrorism network often finds a nexus. It's the home of the most brutal and notorious wing of the mafia now, their stock and trade being drugs, importing and exporting heroin and opium and cocaine, and, worse, human trafficking. Women. Young girls.

Their drug connections stretch all the way to Afghanistan, which makes their bedfellows people like the Taliban and Al Qaeda. Washing drug money through Al Qaeda isn't just stupid, it's potentially fatal. But in Calabria, where the government often looks the other way and the large Muslim community protects its own, it has proven to be lucrative.

That doesn't mean local banks will take the money. But Myanmar? That's a different story.

"What did they say?" I asked.

"They were speaking Italian and that other language," Nate said.

"Farsi?"

"Yeah, yeah," he said, "so I had to call in another favor to get the recording translated. Well, the Italian. I don't know anyone who speaks that other stuff."

"I do," I said, meaning, I do.

"Anyway, again, no rush, but if you could look into a problem this cute waitress I know from Mario's Bit of Italy is having with her landlord, we'd have access to a translator whenever we needed it."

We. This was the peril involved. *We.*

"I speak Italian, too," I said.

"You do?"

"I do," I said. "But I'll take care of her problem. Just tell me what these businessmen said."

"The part in Italian was something about Dinino. They said basically that if everything went well, they'd do it again the following month, too. And then they started going back and forth between the languages and all my friend could get was something about money, something about caviar and something about coming back in town for the Super Bowl."

"These guys," I said. "You get a name for either of them?"

"Better," Nate said. "They paid me with a credit card."

That was better. And worse, shortly, for them.

Nate gave me the name: Domenic Strabo. He may as well have said John Gotti.

"Good work," I said.

"And one more thing," Nate said. "The big money was on the *Pax Bellicosa* to win, up until about two hours ago. Now even people who put huge coin on that are putting even more money on the *Pax Bellicosa* to lose."

"They're betting both ways?"

"That's what my guy says."

If you want to be sure that a game is fixed, watch the bets. A smart fixer will bet on both sides of the ticket so that if there's any investigation, he can show he was just betting for the sake of betting, that he'd even out on either side.

It's called proportional betting.

In blackjack, it's what's known as the d'Alembert method. Increase your bet after each loss, decrease it after each victory. Played out over a long period, and the odds are you'll end up slightly ahead.

Played out on a single race, like the Hurricane Cup, and it's mostly just to cover your ass.

Which meant Christopher Bonaventura put out

the word, at least to the people he didn't want to anger. Or was putting out his own money as insurance.

Either way, I'd done my job.

"Good work," I said.

"That bit of information came steep," Nate said. "My guy, he's got a brother in prison. Trumped-up charge."

"I'm not busting someone out of prison," I said. "And neither is Slade Switchblade."

"Right," Nate said. "Is Fiona around?"

"Nate," I said.

"Right," Nate said. "I'll talk to Fiona later. Whatever. We'll work it out."

"I appreciate all of this," I said.

"Happy to help," Nate said. And it sounded like he really meant it.

"Do me a favor," I said. "Tonight. Leave me a tape of the recording you made at my place and then get out of town. See if you can take everyone you talked to out of town, too."

"Bro, I can handle myself."

"Domenic Strabo isn't just a foot soldier. You drove one of the heads of the Calabria mafia tonight and, probably, someone linked to Al Qaeda. If either are smart enough to piece together anything before they wind up in a cell, you're likely to wake up from a dirt nap."

"Oh," Nate said.

"There's a couple thousand dollars cut into my

mattress. Take it and have a lovely vacation with all of your friends. You need more money, call me. But don't come back until I tell you you're safe."

It wasn't exactly that I was afraid the Mafia might come after Nate; more that I wasn't sure what Alex Kyle might do if this all blew up and he remained standing.

Not that that was something I thought was in the cards for our new friend.

"Okay," Nate said. "But remember to call me this time. Last time you sent me out of town you left me in Fort Lauderdale for weeks."

"That was miscommunication," I said.

"That was no communication," Nate said.

"I'm working on that," I said. "Now go."

I hung up with Nate, filled Fi in on the salient points—except for the part about the prison break, which I knew she'd gladly take part in and would happily begin planning like she was Martha Stewart with bomb-making skills—and called Sam. "Mikey," he said, "glad you called. We need to talk."

I could barely hear Sam over the sound of gushing wind. "Where are you?"

"Just coming in off the *Pax*," he said. "Listen, change of plans."

"You don't know the plan," I said.

"I know my plan," he said. "One of Gennaro's guys is in the hospital."

"What happened?"

"I had to break his arm."

"Okay," I said.

"And he's probably going to have a bit of a speech impediment thing for a while," Sam said. "Nothing major. You ever bite the tip of your tongue off?"

"No."

"Heals right back. Like a lizard's tail. Anyway, we're heading back in now from another run. Looks like I'm on the team tomorrow. For safety reasons."

"Okay," I said. His voice sounded slightly thick, like he was battling the flu. "You all right?"

"These Swan boats? They're not much for smoothness. Not exactly like being out on the QE Two."

"Dramamine didn't help?"

"Turns out Dramamine and beer aren't the best combination before going out for a spin with Gennaro and his crew." He gave a wet cough and then continued. "You were right about the bugs. I swept the place and found ten of them. And not cheap ones, either. Dinino had that place covered. He knew Gennaro would turn to someone. I left them where they were, told Gennaro to just stay cool, keep doing what he was doing, that we were in control of the situation."

"We are," I said.

"We are?"

I filled him in. "What did you hear from Jimenez?"

"A lot of bitching."

"Anything else?"

"What Nate says jibes. Jimenez says rumor is Dinino is in big. Gambling debts from betting on his own team," Sam said.

"Gennaro was winning," I said.

"That's the thing," Sam said. "Jimenez thinks he's been betting on them to lose."

"And the pictures?"

"They want their money. These guys will bring the pain one way or the other. And that's what they traffic in, you know. Sweet guys."

"Well," I said, "they're gonna get their money." I explained to Sam what Barry was going to do tomorrow. And now that I had Strabo's credit card, I knew there'd be at least one high limit charge going through.

"That's the sort of thing that ends up on the news," Sam said.

"All the better," I said. I looked at my watch. It was already late. "What happened on the water?"

"Yeah," Sam said, "about that. Anyone asks, my name is Viv Finley."

"Chuck isn't available?"

Sam cleared his throat. "That's what we need to talk about."

13

In order to become a Navy SEAL, you typically need to spend thirty months training under the most intense physical and mental stress imaginable. You're not just learning how to parachute out of planes, dive into rough seas holding an M-14 sniper rifle, swim into live combat, blow up boats and fight hand-to-hand, you're learning how to do all of that *at one time*. There's a reason only the best of the best qualify to be SEALs.

Sam Axe was a SEAL.

But that was about a decade and a thousand beers ago.

Now, he's a former SEAL, which means he's got all the know-how, all of the training and will, but his fast-twitch muscles are now more like medium-fast-twitch muscles.

Still, sitting aboard the *Pax Bellicosa* as it banked into the open seas reminded Sam of his old training days. The best part of being a SEAL was the whole teamwork aspect, knowing someone always had your back. It was also fun to go into enemy countries to attack militant forces, but it wouldn't have been nearly as much fun if the rest of the team was a bunch of assholes. No, Sam thought, the spray of the ocean splashing into his face, it was always better if everyone was invested.

Which is why when Sam got on the boat with Gennaro's team, he could tell immediately that one of the six crew members, in addition to Gennaro, wasn't quite with the program.

"Who is this?" he asked Gennaro. He had a thick Irish accent. Gennaro was the only actual Italian on board. His team was cobbled from around the country. The best money could buy . . . a point Sam thought was probably true in both good and bad ways.

"A friend," Gennaro said. "He's providing some security." Gennaro explained that the family was concerned about kidnappings and such, which was a sly bit of truth from Gennaro. The kid was learning.

"Chuck Finley," Sam said and extended his hand to the man, who actually recoiled a step before shaking hands.

"Glynn Wilson," he said quickly, like he didn't want Sam to hear it.

"Glynn has been on my team for over a year," Gennaro said, which Sam thought meant he was to be trusted, which would normally be the case except for that recoil. It made him think of Alex

Kyle's men, all of whom were now familiar with good old Chuck, too. He'd need to get a new name one of these days, but it was sort of like a nice pair of jeans. Once you get them worn in, it doesn't make sense to get a new pair.

Now, as they were cutting through the sea, Sam couldn't shake the sense that things were askew with Mr. Wilson. It's not like he wasn't working hard—god knows they all were, even Sam, shuffling back and forth to either side of the yacht as they swung the sail in and out of the wind—but it was the fact that when Gennaro told them they could take a break, none of the others actually did. They talked amongst themselves about strategy, about reading the wind and the water, trading thoughts with Gennaro. Glynn was right there with them, but he was also working with something in his pocket.

Sam made it a point not to pay much attention to the habits of men's hands while in their pockets unless there was obvious danger, but in this case it wasn't like Glynn was pacing in front of a preschool wearing a trench coat, which made it all the more curious. The more Sam watched Glynn, the more Sam began to think there was something very wrong with the fellow.

So when Gennaro called the team back into action, Sam decided it would be wise to use some of his old training, though this was more the sort of thing he'd learned outside of the SEALs.

If you want to pick someone's pocket, the best method is to employ a team: One or two people to cause a distraction—like a fight or a fall—and another person to actually slip into the mark's pocket or purse for the treasure. Or four people to bump directly into the person from all sides—like on a subway—while a fifth filches away.

None of those options were available to Sam aboard the *Pax Bellicosa*, so if he wanted to find out what was going on in Glynn's pocket, he was going to need to try a less subtle approach.

He was going to have to knock him over.

Casually, of course.

The way a Swan picks up racing speed is by turning the bow of the boat into the wind and raising its large main sail, followed by raising the jib and cutting into the ocean currents. The team shifts side to side to make best use of weight distribution and usually, when there isn't an uninvited guest aboard, it's a choreography of brutal elegance as the team slides back and forth, braces the boat, controls the sails and crashes over the water.

The first time, Sam watched Glynn carefully and saw that he was being very mindful not to bump his pocket while the other men were throwing themselves with abandon. On the second shift a few minutes later, Sam decided he'd find out just what was so important.

As the team scurried across, Sam dropped

an elbow—casually—into Glynn's solar plexus, which caused him to double over in pain as he struggled for breath.

"Oh, crap, sorry," Sam said. He grabbed Glynn and helped him from crumbling down, while at the same time pushing the contents of Glynn's front pocket out with an—accidental, of course— knee to Glynn's thigh which Sam then strafed upward into his hip. If there was nothing of interest to be found in Glynn's pocket, he'd apologize profusely to the poor guy. He really would. As it happened, if Glynn had the benefit of any breath, he would have howled in pain and surprise and he probably would have clamored after his silver BlackBerry, which was now skittering across the deck.

"Oh, let me get that for you," Sam said and dropped Glynn—not so casually—onto the deck, too.

On the screen of the BlackBerry was a series of texts, the last of which said, I THNK HIS NAME IS VJIVL FIMNLERY. No one said it was easy to text one-handed while on a racing yacht, but Sam gave the guy credit for being close with the last name, anyway. And it wouldn't take a CIA linguist to figure out Glynn's finger was just placed one key to the side of his intended spot on the first name, at least. Sam couldn't tell from the other name on the screen who Glynn was texting—it said TNT911, which was about as covert as calling yourself Saddam—but had a feeling it was probably someone working with Christopher Bonaventura. If he'd been fixing things, it reasoned he'd keep someone on the boat's payroll just to make sure things went well.

It was enough evidence for Sam, but if it hadn't been, Glynn's sudden lunge toward him would have sealed the deal. Sam met Glynn with an accidental head butt to the bridge of Glynn's nose, which caused the man to slam his head down rather brutally and to bite down hard on his tongue, severing the tip of it.

Sam actually saw it cleave right off and land on Glynn's shirt. Glynn saw it, too, which caused him to pass out. He fell backwards and Sam could hear the audible snap of Glynn's arm. It wasn't a compound fracture, Sam could tell that much, but by the awkward angle it was clear he wouldn't be playing the violin any time soon.

"Hey, Gene?" Sam said, once it was clear Glynn Wilson wouldn't be getting up on his own accord, and once it was clear the rest of the team was rather perplexed by the bloody mess on the ground in front of them. "Looks like Glynn here had an accident."

Gennaro came over and regarded his teammate. "What happened?"

Sam didn't want to explain the intricacies of their issue in front of everyone, so he said the first thing that came to mind. "He fell," Sam said.

He tried to indicate with his eyes just what that meant. When that didn't elicit any kind of response, he added, "while texting Christopher Bonaventura."

That did the trick.

Late that night, Sam told all of us the gory details—the tongue issue was enough to get even Fiona slightly more agitated than a good fight story normally does—as we sat inside my loft. Down the block, the police were still investigating the untimely demise of Rob Roberge, so the street was lit up with halogens, which made the club goers waiting in line outside my window look surprised and bewildered. I wondered if any of them ever saw the sun.

"Where is Glynn now?" I asked.

"We took him to the hospital," Sam said, "but ten minutes later, he was hailing a cab out front. I followed it to the airport. My guess is he's on his way to Belfast."

"Lovely place this time of year," Fi said. "I'd be happy to go and bring back pieces of him for you, Michael."

"I'll pass this time," I said. "What time do you need to be on the yacht tomorrow, Sam?"

"We push off at noon," he said, "but I've gotta be in the marina at nine. You know what Gennaro said? We win this race, everything works out, he'll cut me a share of the purse."

"That's not going to happen," I said.

"It's not going to work out?"

"No," I said, "you're not sharing the purse. This whole thing is dirty, Sam. Once this race is finished, I have a feeling no one is going to be untouched. Not even Gennaro."

It was the sad truth of it all—if everything I thought we could set in motion actually worked, it would only take one person to roll to implicate Gennaro.

The lucky thing was that one person was Christopher Bonaventura. And he wasn't going to have room to roll. He might try, but it wouldn't do him any good.

"Your friend in the FBI might be interested in requisitioning a boat for herself," I said. "Because I think she's going to have a chance to bring down Christopher Bonaventura in a rather large kidnapping for hire scheme involving the Ottone family."

Our plan was going to be deceptively simple: Make Christopher Bonaventura's men board the Ottone yacht forcefully. They'd be doing it for the right reasons—to save Maria and Liz—but for the wrong motivation, namely to keep Bonaventura from a murder rap. I had a feeling that Maria and Liz probably weren't actually being held captive. It was Dinino's ploy to convince Gennaro, but it seemed like an unlikely truth at the moment. Dinino wasn't a crook. He was a businessman. A smart businessman. And a smart businessman doesn't have a boat full of killers at his disposal. He might have cameras. He might have a tech guy. But if he wanted to pull off this ruse to get out of his girl problems, like anyone else, he would limit the number of people on his team.

If Maria and Liz had to die, he'd figure out a way to do it himself. Which meant poison, or drowning or something far less personal—or trackable—than a gunshot.

"Darleen will appreciate that," Sam said, which I took to mean Sam would appreciate the contact again. I guess he still wanted to clear some possible misconceptions up. "And those pictures you have of Dinino and the girl? Make a thousand photocopies?"

"No," I said. "I think we should time an e-mail to go out at about noon tomorrow. All the papers in Italy should do the trick, right?"

"Just send it to one of those gossip blogs," Fiona said. "It will be around the world in twenty seconds."

She was right. It would only take moments for Dinino to be cut out of his own family. The speed of the Internet would convict him long before a court. And the men he was dealing with would have their own justice, too.

"What about the girl?" I said.

"It would be the best thing for her," Fiona said. "If she's been used, the authorities will be able to keep her safe."

Maybe. For good measure, we'd send her photo to the FBI, too.

"See," Sam said, "you're a friendly guy. Helping out someone you don't even know and will never meet. It's a nice way of building relationships, Mikey. I bet in no time you'll be just like me. Friends in every corner of the universe. Help your reputation in international circles. Maybe prevent a couple attempts on your life."

"I don't see that happening."

"Just saying," Sam said.

"Were you able to get me a boat for tomorrow from Virgil?" I said, speaking of friends I didn't want.

"Yeah. About that. Virgil said he got a good deal on a classic. Said it isn't sleek, but it's fast."

"Sam," I said.

"It'll be fine," he said. "You can depend on Virgil."

It was true. I just didn't want to have to.

"We just need something that can close a gap if a problem goes down," I said. "Fi, you comfortable with this?"

"I'm comfortable knowing that tomorrow at this time I may have shot at something," she said.

"Well, anyway, Virgil's happy to help," Sam said.

"He's not coming, is he?"

"Well, that was part of the deal," Sam said. "I told him it was an important mission. He's good in a fight, Mikey."

True enough. But Virgil was also one of the people who attracted problems. And my mom.

"I'd like to avoid feeling . . . *uncomfortable*," I said.

"I hear you," Sam said.

I didn't think he actually did, but it was a moot point now. Virgil was coming.

"When did Gennaro last talk to his wife?"

"This evening. She still thinks everything is fine."

"Good," I said. "If she never knows, even better."

"Mikey," he said, "listen. You get into international waters tomorrow, and Alex Kyle will take his shot."

"I know that," I said.

"And maybe ten or twenty others."

"I know that, too," I said.

Outside, the halogens clicked off and the once bright street fell into its usual darkness, which meant it still had the periodic blue glow from inside the club, but was otherwise now just a street, not a crime scene. Whoever had taken out Rob Roberge didn't even want him *thinking* of hurting me, much less doing anything to hurt me. If I left the waters of the United States, it wouldn't just be the people who burned me who'd be upset, it would possibly be plenty of other organizations, both known and unknown, who would scramble the appropriate response.

I needed to make this happen tomorrow with a minimum of collateral damage, to say nothing of sparing my own life.

"He'll wear floaties," Fi said to Sam, "in case I need to throw him overboard."

14

A popular misconception is that spies are always armed. The spies we all know—James Bond, Napoleon Solo, Jim Phelps, even Maxwell Smart—didn't just have guns, they also had cigarette cases that turned into grenade launchers, belt buckles that were also lasers, cars that doubled as nuclear submarines, watches that contained antishark sonar and tuxedos that morphed into rocket packs.

The truth is that spies are rarely armed. Operate in a country like China and be found with a gun on your person and you're going to prison. Chinese prison. Get found in Russia with a gun on you, you're likely to find yourself breaking ice in Siberia.

Gun laws in Florida aren't exactly friendly, either. No American state looks kindly on people shooting up city blocks, and diplomatic cloak only goes so far if you happen to embarrass the right people. Generally, the government doesn't want its people to be aware of the fact that counterintelligence is going on right under their nose. Get arrested for carrying in Miami and you're likely to stay in jail until your handler can figure out a way to fake your death. You'll get out eventually, but it might be no easy task.

Being a burned spy carries no such assurances of safety from criminal prosecution. Shoot someone in broad daylight and people are going to ask questions.

I might have guardian angels, as Alex Kyle said, but even they answered to someone; someone who likely would not want to answer to widespread carnage on the streets of Miami.

Use a gun in international or domestic waters, however, and it's an entirely different standard, particularly if you're on one boat and the person you're shooting at is on another. You can be tried as a pirate. Contrary to Jimmy Buffett songs and Disney movies, this is not a good thing.

Piracy laws over the course of the last five years have been modified so that you're not just committing maritime crimes, you're actually being looked at under a standard normally reserved for terrorists.

Which is why I wasn't about to put myself in that situation. But was happy to put Alex Kyle and Christopher Bonaventura there.

It was eleven forty five a.m. and Biscayne Bay was filled with boats—pleasure yachts, sailboats, catamarans—and revelers. The marina at the South-

ern Cross Yacht Club was alive with partygoers.
The Hurricane Cup, racing from Miami to Nassau
over the course of two days, was a traveling party.
It started here, in Miami, and over the next
twenty-four hours on the open sea, boat to boat, it
kept on.

The course was buoyed so the racers would
know where to go and the partyers would know
where to park. From Miami to Nassau harbor,
drinks would roll down throats, money would
change hands, and for most people worth millions
of dollars, nothing would seem untoward.

Sam was aboard the *Pax Bellicosa*, but someone
important was missing. "Dinino is nowhere," Sam
said when he called from the marina.

"What do you mean nowhere?" I asked.

"Gennaro says he's always right in the marina
for a launch, playing the big guy, but he's not
here."

It didn't make sense. He would either be watching the race or . . .

Up above, I heard the familiar *whoop-whoop* of a
helicopter—there were several in the air covering
the event, which made things even more likely to be
newsworthy today—and a thought occurred to me.

"Why don't you ask Gennaro if the family has a
helicopter," I said.

"You think he's flying to the Ottone yacht?"

"That would be my play. Kill the girls himself if
he has to."

"Not even Bonaventura would let him do that," Sam said.

"That's the hope," I said. In the background, I heard an announcement telling all the racers to make final preparations. "You better get moving."

"Right. And hey, Mikey?"

"Yeah Sam?"

"If it turns out everything is aces here," he said, "I'm just letting you know I'm prepared to give a portion of my cut of the winnings to a charity of your choice."

"Still not happening," I said and hung up. The reality of the situation was that I wasn't convinced Gennaro could win on his own regardless. Once everyone was safe, once he knew his wife and child would be fine and that he wasn't looking at running from Christopher Bonaventura the rest of his life, the odds were that he'd relax, lose that laser focus of fear and would probably just race.

In a fairytale, he'd win. But I felt I knew Gennaro now and if he said he wasn't as good as the best on the water, I was inclined to believe him.

A large, all black party boat came up along our stern, rock music blaring. I looked and saw bodies writhing on the top deck. It was as if a nightclub sprung out of the clear blue ocean. No one seemed the least bit concerned about anything, which is perhaps because they hadn't yet noticed the rickety boat from the mid-1970s floating nearby, the only passengers Fiona and me . . . and Virgil.

"Thanks for inviting me to the party," Virgil said.

"My pleasure," I said.

We'd departed from South Beach hours before but were just a few miles outside Government Cut, waiting for the racers to launch and come our way. They all moved at the same leisurely pace until they hit the open water and then the competition actually began. The first leg out of Miami was strictly show. A floating nightclub would only go so far. Right here was about the limit.

Our main goal was just to locate the Ottones' yacht. Now more than ever, with the idea that Dinino might be aboard, I needed to make sure Bonaventura's men got there. They might kill Dinino, but they'd never touch Maria and Liz.

The yacht was due to come through this shipping lane any moment now en route to the mouth of Government Cut for Maria to see her husband, which was her ritual. There was only another eight miles of sea between here and international waters, which meant I had a very narrow amount of ground to work in. I was confined to Miami by the government, but I was also confined by my enemies.

Both would shoot me.

Not much of a party.

"How's your mom doing?"

"Good," I said.

"I haven't been able to see her for a bit," Virgil

said. "I've been doing some business in Pensacola."

"Good," I said. Fi and I were looking through binoculars now for any site of the Ottones' ship. If Maria and Liz were going to be at Government Cut in time for Gennaro to stream by, that meant Bonaventura was likely to make his move immediately, too. All he needed to do was secure the ship.

And that would be enough to get him arrested.

But I needed to be there in case something, anything, went wrong. I'd promised Gennaro his wife and child would be safe and I wasn't going to leave it solely in the hands of Christopher Bonaventura, or Alex Kyle, to make that happen. Plus, as soon as Alex Kyle saw us coming close, he was sure to redouble his efforts to stop the Ottones' ship.

"She said you two were going to start doing more bonding exercises," Virgil said.

"Uh-huh."

"Just want you to know I am in absolute support of that," he said. "Man to man. It's good to have positive relationships with your mama. Know what I mean?"

"Virgil," I said, "no offense? But this isn't a conversation I really want to have with you right now."

"No problem, Mike," he said. He put a big paw on my shoulder. "Whenever you want to talk."

He walked back to the front of the boat and I kept my eyes on the water, as did Fi.

Everyone was silent for a time.

"He's just trying to be kind, Michael," Fi said.

"Not talking about this," I said.

"You know, that's your prone position, Michael," Fi said. "It's like that fellow from Target. What was his name?"

"Davey," I said.

"Right. Now there was a person just trying to connect with you and you were just rude to him."

"Fiona," I said, "can't this wait?"

"All we're doing is staring at the sea. We can talk and stare."

"Fine," I said.

"Fine," she said. Now she was mad. It's never easy to work with people you used to sleep with. She was silent again for a time. Virgil was now spitting dip into a small cup, which I guess is how he relaxes in tense situations. "I'm just saying," she continued, "that it would be nice if every now and then you admitted that it was your fault when lines of communication break down."

"Are we talking about us or about my mother and I or about me and Virgil?" I said.

"All of it," she said.

"Fine," I said. I was scanning back and forth across the horizon, as was Fiona, which was good since that way we didn't have to look at each other. "From now on, I'm an open book."

"I'd find that more convincing if..." she stopped. "Five o'clock. Do you see that?"

Cutting through the water was a gold Chris-Craft Cobra speedboat. I trained my binoculars on it. I couldn't make out faces, but I could tell there were five men on the boat and none of them had body types that screamed *pleasure seekers.*

"Virgil," I shouted, "that's our target."

He put down his dip cup and came next to me. "Fast son of a bitch."

"It's from this century and everything," I said.

The best boat to have in a situation like this would be a boat made for stealth tracking. Something like a Night Cat, a twenty-seven-foot boat with twin 300 horsepower engines that purr instead of roar, so that the person you're tracking doesn't get the impression that a Nimitz Class is on their ass. A Night Cat can turn at 41 degrees per second, which makes it about as responsive as the muscles that make you blink.

But that would only be if you didn't want to be seen. I needed Alex Kyle to see me. To know we were making our move on Maria and Liz.

"Let's rock and roll!" Virgil bellowed and gunned the engine, or as much as you can gun an engine on a fourteen-foot Pinecraft whose best days were probably pre-disco. A plume of blue smoke belched from the engine and a sound like an entire NASCAR race starting soon followed.

The men on the Cobra turned their heads. It was that loud. And that was fine.

"Don't worry," Virgil said. "Once she gets moving, she moves."

"Ship on the horizon," Fi said. "Six o'clock. Practically the size of an island."

Through my binoculars I could see a boat of at least four hundred feet in length. It was black from the waterline, its steel hull looming with uncommon grace. Above the hull were five floors of living space (and likely, entertainment) space. The floors were a blinding white, which gave the entire ship the appearance of a tuxedo in the water.

"You need to get that Cobra as close to that ship as possible; push it right into its line," I said to Virgil.

"That wasn't part of the deal Sam put out," Virgil said. "I thought we were just intercepting."

"We are," I said. "And pushing."

"I'd like to avoid jail time for causing a death on the sea," Virgil said.

"Not going to happen," I said. "All we want is for the men in that Cobra to stop the Ottones' ship and board it. You get that Cobra into a position to make that happen."

Virgil smiled. "You're a devious man, Mike."

I checked my watch. The time was now. We had calls and e-mails to send. I called Gennaro. I had five minutes before he'd launch. "I can see your wife's boat," I said.

"Is she safe?"

"She will be."

"What do I do?"

"Race," I said. "Just race. Win or lose. It's on you alone now."

"And my wife is safe?"

"Yes," I said. Now I just had to make sure it happened. Gennaro put Sam on the phone. "Tell Darleen these coordinates," I said and rattled off our location. A woman like Darleen was already waiting somewhere out in the water, so it would only be a matter of moments, I was certain, for this to all happen.

"Got it, Mikey," he said. "Be safe."

"What fun is that?" I said. "See you after you get back from Nassau."

I called Barry and told him to begin the flood. In minutes, a crime family with terrorist connections, that Nicholas Dinino was transferring large sums of cash to, which was probably placing large sums of money in illegal betting on the *Pax Bellicosa* losing, would be under investigation by every bank in the world.

"Send the pictures," I said to Fiona, which she did from her cell phone. In a few seconds, Nicholas Dinino wouldn't just be in trouble with the mob and terrorists, he'd be in the process of get-

ting cut out of the Ottone empire, probably before
he ever saw land again.

We'd caught Nicholas Dinino. Now it was
about finishing the race.

The difference between chasing someone and
intercepting someone is all about angles. When
you chase someone, you're naturally in a passive
position. You can only act when they act. You have
no control over the flow of the chase.

But when you're intercepting someone, you dictate the angle of pursuit. Which is why instead of
trying to catch Alex Kyle's Cobra from behind, we
were actively pushing it toward Ottones' ship, cutting across the water at a 45-degree angle, so that
we would T-bone the Cobra. The goal was to ensure not that they were forced to engage us, but
that they were forced to make the Ottones' ship
stop, that they would board the ship to protect
Maria and Liz, likely find Nicholas Dinino, and,
if all happened in good timing, do so in front of
the FBI.

But first it had to happen.

We sliced through the water, the front of the
boat bouncing into the air as we crossed over
whitecaps, the Cobra coming clearer into view, the
Ottones' ship looming larger in the distance.

And then my cell phone rang.

It wasn't a number I recognized.

"You're getting very close to the edge," a
woman's voice said when I answered.

"Not much farther," I said.

"You have three minutes." This time it was a man.

I tossed the phone into the water.

"Your mother?" Fi said.

"No," I said.

She dug into a cabinet at her feet and pulled out a life vest. "Put your floaties on," she said.

"I'm fine," I said.

The Cobra was now only about fifty yards from us, close enough that I could make out the faces of the men on board. It was easier when Alex Kyle turned and smiled at me. The Cobra banked left, then right, trying to shake us but Virgil's little engine could and we kept up, drawing closer to their flank.

The Ottones' ship let out a bellow. We were both getting perilously close to it at this point.

Virgil looked back at me, worry on his face. "Go," I said. "We have to make this happen or everyone dies."

It was a fact I hadn't quite considered, but that was seeming more and more true, now that I could make out a helipad on the bow of the Ottones' yacht, a forest green chopper sitting at rest.

I was certain it was Nicholas Dinino.

If I didn't get Alex Kyle and his men on that ship, there was no stopping Bonaventura from exacting vengeance, sometime, somewhere, for all of this. And if those men didn't get on the ship, there

was a good chance Dinino would kill Maria and
Liz. Bonaventura most likely told Kyle to watch
the boat, make sure I didn't board it. Make sure I
didn't kill anyone.

Alex Kyle knew the truth. He knew what I was
capable of and what I was unlikely to do, but he
was following orders. We had to make it look like
we were heading for that boat to do what we had
to do.

Overhead, I heard the whooping of helicopters.
The sky was alive with them now, television coverage beaming images around the world, but
there's a different sound between the nice chop-
pers TV stations use and military transports.

Alex Kyle looked up, too, and pointed. And
then turned and pointed at me, like a warning.

And maybe it was.

Fi's cell phone rang.

"Don't answer it," I said.

Virgil's cell phone rang and he just tossed it
overboard. "I got the message," he said.

The Ottones' ship bellowed again. We had
twenty yards between us and the Cobra, another
three hundred before we were in the path of the
cruise liner.

"Turn," I said very calmly to Virgil, "put us
right in the path of the ship."

"We'll have maybe fifteen seconds and that's
it," he said. "This girl doesn't do tricks."

"That's all we need," I said.

Virgil spun our boat towards the Ottones' ship.

My assumption was that the ship's captain would make the only correction he could—back towards the Cobra, which it did. The Cobra was a gymnast; it would be able to draw back and around the big ship without a problem.

Well, some problems.

"Get us out," I yelled to Virgil and he cranked us back towards Miami, the boat lurching, the engine spitting out more blue smoke into the air.

We could hear the engine on the Ottones' ship sputtering. If the captain were smart—and if the Ottones' employed him and he wasn't in the tank to kill Maria and Liz, he was—he'd throw the engine into reverse and kill it, stopping the forward momentum as much as possible. Which is what it sounded like was happening as the engines of the big yacht ground audibly, the captain trying to get it to decelerate any way he could.

The Cobra was fast enough to get out of the way and then circled back around the lumbering ship. I watched the Cobra pacing the cruise liner, which had slowed considerably. Through the binoculars I could see Alex on the radio and his men standing upright with shoulder-fired spearguns aimed above the hull of the ship. They were dressed to rappel, which meant they were planning to board shortly.

"It's too bad," Fiona said.

"What is?" I said.

"That Alex Kyle fellow," she said. "He seemed like the kind of person we might like in a different situation."

"Maybe he'll come back and try to sell some plutonium," I said. I was still watching when he gave the signal and his men fired their spears into the deck of the boat. They weren't shooting to harm, but to set up rappelling lines. Within seconds, Kyle's teams was scaling the side of the hull.

"Nice form," Virgil said.

"We never get to do fun things like that," Fi said.

"I have a feeling this will be the last time these men get the chance," I said. Just then a military helicopter swept down in front of the ship and hovered above the stern. Another came to the bow. There were three in the air now and I could make out a Coast Guard cutter screaming in from the east, another from the south. "I think they've just acted as pirates in the service of a Mafia boss."

Fi's phone began to ring and she handed it to me.

I looked at the caller ID. Restricted. Big surprise.

"Hello?" I said, as chummy as possible.

"Stay," said the woman's voice. "Enjoy the race."

"I think I will," I said and then tossed the phone into the sea.

Epilogue

When you're no longer a spy, it's important to understand that the people you love sometimes need to know that you, belatedly, are willing to deal with some of life's larger issues with them.

Which is precisely what I was doing while sitting in the offices of Dr. Helen Miyazawa. My mother, Madeline, was sitting to one side of me, an unlit cigarette between her fingers. A stuffed Snoopy, portraying my father, was on the other side of me, and Dr. Miyazawa paced the room. Or at least I think she paced the room. It was hard to tell because all the lights in the office were off and the only illumination in the room came from a flashlight shot through a green marble on the doctor's desk, which made everything look vaguely like a cave in Tora Bora at sunrise.

It was a week after the race and if Sam's friend Darleen was to be believed, I'd brought down Christopher Bonaventura and Alex Kyle, saved the Ottone family empire, helped capture the banking information and funds of an international terrorist network and likely imprisoned Nicholas Dinino for life.

Or, as Sam told it, since he didn't want to involve me too directly, he'd done all of that.

I had to believe what Darleen told Sam because none of this appeared on the news or in the papers, or even on any blogs. Well, except for the photos of Nicholas Dinino and the young girl. She was a minor star now in Europe, probably would have a recording deal within a month and be forgotten in two. Gone. Disappeared.

Just like Nicholas Dinino, a man I'd never actually met, but who probably wishes he never even heard my name on a recording.

There's a difference, however, between disappearing and being disappeared. You help the FBI with evidence against crime families, you tend to get special treatment, and though Darleen didn't say so, I was inclined to believe that Nicholas Dinino was probably in a safe house in Phoenix, giving the FBI all the information he could to save his ass.

And the *Pax Bellicosa*? It came in fifth. On its own, it still lost. And Sam spent twenty-four hours working harder than he had in twenty years. When he came back to America three days later, after some "Sam Time" with what he called "race groupies" he still had blisters on all of his fingers.

All that had been accomplished, and yet I still

had to bond with my mother, and it was somehow far more difficult. If things didn't improve, I thought that it was only a matter of time before I woke up one morning to find Dr. Phil standing in my kitchen, eating my yogurt.

"Tell me, Michael," Dr. Miyazawa said from somewhere in her office I couldn't quite pinpoint, "what would you say to your father right now if he were sitting beside you?"

"Honestly?"

"Yes, yes, of course," she said.

"I'd ask him to shoot me."

"Michael!" my mother said.

"No, no, this is good, Mrs. Westen," Dr. Miyazawa said. "Go ahead, Michael. Why would you ask him to shoot you?"

I had the vague sense she might actually be beneath her desk. If I'd known this was all going to happen under the cloak of darkness, I would have brought night-vision goggles with me. The week prior, just days after the events of the Hurricane Cup, the three of us actually met out on the beach so the doctor could perform a clarifying ceremony, which involved my mother screaming into the ocean for ten minutes about all of the terrible things I'd ever done to her. Next week there was a field trip scheduled to an ashram in Boynton Beach, where we were to bond over the spiritual revelations.

"Well," I said, finally answering the question,

"the muzzle flash would probably get you to turn on the lights, for one, which would give me an opportunity to look at your diploma a little closer, see where exactly you learned that trick with the marble."

"Many of my clients find the marble light very comforting," she said. "You don't find it comforting?"

"No."

"What do you find comforting, Michael?"

"Building explosives."

"Do you often think about dying, Michael? Do you feel obsessed with your own demise? Do you feel that your father has, in some way, killed you before, turned you into a shell of a person?"

I checked my watch. We had about ten more minutes of this. "Yeah," I said. "It was either him or my unborn twin."

"Michael," my mother said, "you know that's not true. You never had an unborn twin."

"You're right," I said. "I'm also not a shell of a person, and I'm beginning to strongly doubt Dr. Miyazawa is an actual doctor, so we're all on an even playing field now."

Dr. Miyazawa sighed. That was her go-to sound. I still couldn't really see her. "We haven't talked about this before, but you two might be perfect candidates for a birth reenactment."

"I understand why Medicare won't pay for these appointments," I said.

"Do you ever get tired of using sarcasm as a defense?" Dr. Miyazawa asked.

"Sarcasm is actually a very advanced brain function," I said, which was the launching point for my mother to go into an exceptionally involved story about some perceived sarcasm-based injustice done upon her by me when I was six, which led Dr. Miyazawa to ask my mother about her feelings concerning any past lives I might have had and then, well, I just stopped listening completely. When people start arguing past lives, it's only a matter of time until someone has tarot cards on the table.

I closed my eyes and tried to imagine other instances of torture that were worse than this one, see if I couldn't localize the pain into a single trauma in my past versus actually being present in the current one. Of course, it was just as easy to ruminate on the larger arc of my life, which, at present was more like a flatline with the occasional spike along the way. So maybe the EKG of my life would be more accurate, at least since finding out a little more than a year ago that I'd been burned, my spy status turned inside out by forces beyond my control. Forces that in the last week had shown me yet again how powerless I could be.

"Do you agree, Michael?"

I opened my eyes at the sound of Dr. Miyazawa's voice. She and my mother stared at me intently. At some point, the lights had been turned on, which was nice, because now I could actually see my accuser again. She was sitting on a rolling stool in the middle of the room, her hands folded atop her lap on a notebook that she'd apparently been writing in while I pondered the fate of my existence. Or maybe she was just doing Mad Libs. Either way, I didn't have any idea what the doctor was querying me about, but I knew the answer.

"No," I said.

"Why is that?" she asked.

"Why is what?"

Dr. Miyazawa exhaled through her mouth and nodded at my mother, as if my answer confirmed some especially salient point. She scooted across the room on her stool until she was only inches away from me. "I'd like you to pretend I'm your father," she said.

"No, you wouldn't," I said.

"Tell me why you're angry at me," she said. She deepened her voice, which made her sound sort of like a fifty-something Japanese woman with a head cold. Not quite dear old Dad.

I leaned forward and patted Dr. Miyazawa on the knee. "Here's the problem, Doctor," I said. "You're sweet, really. I think that you're probably exceptionally qualified to help people who want to be helped. But if you want to do role-playing with me, it would probably be more effective if you put a knife to my throat and asked me where the secret documents were. At least then I'd be doing something enjoyable."

"Michael," Mom said, "she's just trying to help us bond. You could indulge her."

Mom turned away from me and addressed the doctor, her voice dropping to a conspiratorial level. "The doctors wanted Michael put into a body cast," she said. "He had terrible scoliosis. He probably doesn't remember that. Probably blacked that out entirely."

"That's entirely possible," Dr. Miyazawa said.

"I can hear you, Ma," I said.

"I can still see the X-ray," Mom said. Her eyes welled with tears.

"Here we go," I said.

"His spine looked like a U."

"That explains a great deal," Dr. Miyazawa said. "Michael, do you remember any of this?"

Yes, I wanted to say. *Yes, I remember it being a scene in* Looking for Mr. Goodbar. But for some reason I just didn't have the heart. Here we were, sitting in this woman's office, talking about feelings neither of us probably ever had, certainly not making new memories, as was the original proviso, and absolutely not bonding.

I stood up. "Ma," I said, "why don't we go shopping for some linens. And some towels. I could probably use some dishes, too. A few cups and saucers would be good. Fiona likes tea."

"Really? You want to do that? With me?"

"I do," I said. "It's time I got a bit more comfortable here."

"Oh, Michael, I'd love that."

If I'd learned anything, it was that I wasn't going anywhere soon, and wasn't going anywhere fast. I didn't think a trip to Sears would fix four decades of weirdness with my mother, nor stop me from looking over my shoulder for the people who burned me, but for one day, it might just make someone happy and that, well, that wasn't something I did every day, as a spy or as a son.

We walked out of the office without another word to Dr. Miyazawa, who was nonetheless spouting some theory about re-creating the placenta through retail therapy being a false hope. Outside, the air was warm and you could smell the ocean blowing in on the wind.

And a black SUV, the windows tinted, the doors clearly armored, pulled slowly out of a parking space next to my Charger and inched out into the midafternoon traffic. On my windshield was an envelope.

"Is that a ticket?" my mother asked.

"Yes," I said. I opened the envelope and looked inside. There was a slip of paper with a single sentence written on it in thick black marker. *Don't get too comfortable.*